MW00366099

Praise for
New York Times and USA Today Bestselling Author
Diane Capri

"Full of thrills and tension, but smart and human, too."
*Lee Child, #1 World Wide Bestselling Author of Jack Reacher
Thrillers*

"[A] welcome surprise….[W]orks from the first page
to 'The End'."
Larry King

"Swift pacing and ongoing suspense are always
present…[L]ikable protagonist who uses her political
connections for a good cause…Readers should eagerly anticipate
the next [book]."
Top Pick, Romantic Times

"…offers tense legal drama with courtroom overtones, twisty
plot, and loads of Florida atmosphere. Recommended."
Library Journal

"[A] fast-paced legal thriller…energetic prose…an appealing
heroine…clever and capable supporting cast…[that will] keep
readers waiting for the next [book]."
Publishers Weekly

"Expertise shines on every page."
*Margaret Maron, Edgar, Anthony, Agatha and Macavity Award
Winning MWA Past President*

RESERVATION
WITH
DEATH

by DIANE CAPRI

Copyright © 2019 Diane Capri, LLC
All Rights Reserved

All rights reserved as permitted under the U.S. Copyright Act of 1976. No part of the publication may be reproduced, distributed, or transmitted in any form or by any means, or stored in a database or retrieval system, without the prior permission of the publisher. The only exception is brief quotation in printed reviews.

Published by: AugustBooks
http://www.AugustBooks.com

ISBN: 978-1-942633-25-9

Original cover design by: Dar Albert
Digital formatting by: Author E.M.S.
Interior cat silhouettes used under CC0 license from openclipart.org.

Reservation with Death is a work of fiction. Names, characters, places, and incidents either are the product of the author's imagination or are used fictitiously, and any resemblance to actual persons, living or dead, business establishments, events, or locales is entirely coincidental.

Published in the United States of America.

Visit the author website:
http://www.DianeCapri.com

ALSO BY DIANE CAPRI

The Park Hotel Mysteries Series
Reservation with Death
Early Check Out
Room with a Clue
Late Arrival

The Hunt for Justice Series
Due Justice
Twisted Justice
Secret Justice
Wasted Justice
Raw Justice
Mistaken Justice (*novella*)
Cold Justice (*novella*)
False Justice (*novella*)
Fair Justice (*novella*)
True Justice (*novella*)
Night Justice

The Heir Hunter Series
Blood Trails
Trace Evidence

Jordan Fox Mysteries Series
False Truth
(An 11-book continuity series)

The Hunt for Jack Reacher Series:
(in publication order with Lee Child source books in parentheses)
Don't Know Jack (The Killing Floor)
Jack in a Box (*novella*)
Jack and Kill (*novella*)
Get Back Jack (Bad Luck & Trouble)
Jack in the Green (*novella*)
Jack and Joe (The Enemy)
Deep Cover Jack (Persuader)
Jack the Reaper (The Hard Way)
Black Jack (Running Blind/The Visitor)
Ten Two Jack (The Midnight Line)
Jack of Spades (Past Tense)

The Jess Kimball Thrillers Series
Fatal Enemy (*novella*)
Fatal Distraction
Fatal Demand
Fatal Error
Fatal Fall
Fatal Edge (*novella*)
Fatal Game
Fatal Bond
Fatal Past (*novella*)
Fatal Dawn

RESERVATION
WITH
DEATH

CHAPTER ONE

FINDING A DEAD BODY stuffed in the utility room at the Park Hotel pool was not the way I'd anticipated my new life would roll out. Not by a long shot. My fallback job had only just begun, and it was already filled with turmoil. I would have stuck with being a lawyer, but they'd kicked me out. Every time I thought about it, which was too often, the unfairness of it all gave me heartburn.

I'd been suspended. Indefinitely. Thinking I was going to be offered a low-level partnership after six long years, I'd walked into the meeting with the managing partners feeling excited and nervous at the same time.

"Sit down, Andi," Richard Chambers had told me, gesturing to one of the chairs across the long conference table. "We need to talk. About Rucker."

I blinked twice at Derek, the senior managing partner of Alcott, Chambers & Rucker. He was the Alcott. He pointed at the empty chair as if I was a little thick or something. Since my knees were a bit wobbly, I slid into the suggested chair and put my hands in my lap. There was a slight tremble in my hands that I wouldn't allow them to see.

Which was when Richard accused me of helping Jeremy Rucker, my boss and the third managing partner, embezzle several million dollars from the firm's clients. "Where did you stash the money, Ms. Steele?"

"I'm a-afraid I don't q-quite understand the q-question," I stammered. I did understand, of course. I'd worked closely with Jeremy. It wasn't a big leap for them to accuse me of being in cahoots with the thief. Still, it was shocking to hear the words. I stalled to get my thoughts in order so I didn't babble like an incompetent moron.

There were stacks of files on the table. The top file belonged to Beatrice Sorokin. She was one of the firm's long-time clients. Her entire estate had been entrusted to us. I had worked with Jeremy on her account. Seeing her name there made it all too real. The life I'd built for myself was crashing down around me, and there wasn't a damn thing I could do to stop it.

"You were aware that Jeremy was stealing money from client accounts and funneling it into offshore accounts of his own, were you not?" Derek asked.

What? Are you kidding me?

"Absolutely not," I said as calmly as I could. Sweat trickled down my neck and under the collar of my blouse. Fifteen more minutes and I was definitely going to have a sweat stain the size and shape of Texas on my back.

"You were aware that he had a gambling problem, of course. He couldn't possibly have hidden that from you. You worked on every single one of his client matters. You traveled out of town together. You *had* to know." This from Richard, who had that look on his face. It didn't matter what I said. He believed I'd known what Jeremy was doing at the very least…and most likely participated.

"No, I wasn't. Aware, that is. I didn't know." Although I was pretty certain Jeremy had a stack of scratch-and-win lotto cards in his desk drawer. When I said "stack," I meant a mini-mountain of over a hundred. I'd mentioned the cards to him once, and he waved it off as just a bit of fun. Something he did to relax. Who knew the silly lotto cards were a gateway to something more ominous? Not me.

So I didn't know what Jeremy was doing. I've always been nosy by nature. I *have* to know what's going on. At all times. I love to figure things out and to fix them. I try to see things others miss. I check everything twice. Make sure I've dotted every "i" and crossed every "t". Every time. Partly, this is the way I control the unpredictable nature of life. I try to see the bad stuff coming straight at me like a speeding bullet. These are perfect character traits for a lawyer, after all. Which is why I'd been so good at my job. So looking back on it, I kicked myself because I *should* have known about Jeremy. Shouldn't I have? Hindsight is always twenty-twenty. But still.

Derek put his hand on the stack of files. "Ms. Steele, we've been through the files for all of Jeremy's clients. For those he defrauded, you performed legal work on one hundred percent of those matters. You couldn't *possibly* have been in the dark about this."

"Well, I do work for Jeremy. So it makes sense that I dealt with his clients in some capacity." I was stalling because that's all I could do.

"It's precisely that capacity we're trying to work out," Richard said, no humor in his tone at all. Like I was a five-year-old being chastised by her daddy for serious transgressions and no excuse would ever suffice.

"What does Jeremy say?" I was afraid to ask the question, but I had to know if he had thrown me under the bus. How much trouble was I in? I'd probably be smart to retain a good lawyer. I groaned.

They glanced at each other, and then Derek replied, "He really hasn't said much at this point."

"There will be an investigation," Richard said, "You'll need to make a statement."

"I understand."

"And you'll take some time off," Derek said, leaving me no wiggle room.

I looked from Derek to Richard, a lump forming in my throat. All I ever wanted to be was a lawyer. I watched old reruns of lawyer shows on late night TV. Stuff like Perry Mason and Matlock. I grew up laughing at Ally McBeal, promising myself never to be as careless with the law or with clients as she was. I had a poster of Gregory Peck as Atticus Finch on my bedroom wall. I'd worked hard in law school to graduate summa cum laude. I was good at my job. I loved my job. I *was* my job. And now...now they had yanked everything away from me for no fault of my own.

"Are you f-firing me?" The question came out as incredulously as I felt.

Derek put his hand up, palm out. "We didn't say that. You are suspended without pay while these allegations are investigated. We have no choice."

I stood, anger making my knees ramrod straight. "I don't think so."

"I'm sorry?" Derek frowned.

"You can't suspend me. You have no evidence that I did anything wrong. Because I didn't. Jeremy may have taken client money. I don't know. But not me. I. Did. Not. Do. That."

"Now, Andi…" Richard started, but I didn't let him finish.

"Call any of those clients, and they will tell you my work is exemplary." Using my fingers, I started ticking off my reasons. "For the past six years, I've never, ever missed a deadline. Never had a client complaint of any sort. I've worked twelve hours a day, six to seven days a week. I've worked holidays. Never taken off more than two consecutive days at a time, and the only time I did was for my grandma's funeral in Michigan. I've devoted my life to this firm and to the law, and I won't be pushed out for something over which I had zero control."

It was a nice speech. It got me nowhere. They held all the power.

But it made me feel better. Which I suppose was a small victory.

Derek and Richard remained firm. They suspended me from work. They assured me I wouldn't be disbarred and never allowed to practice law again. Not yet, anyway.

I held my head high and walked out of the boardroom with dignity intact. *Never let them see you sweat, baby girl,* my nanny Miss Charlotte always used to say when I was nervous about something. Problem was my blouse was already soaked with sweat and sticking to me.

They'd emptied my desk and packed up my stuff. All of it fit into a single box. They took my parking pass. And the glass door to the entrance of the firm actually swung back before I could get all the way outside and smacked me in the ass. Whatever.

"Damn it, Jeremy!" I shouted to no one when I got outside. But I was mostly angry at myself. How oblivious could an experienced lawyer be?

They were right. I should've known he was embezzling.
There must've been signs. I should've taken a closer look at our
client files. Maybe I would've seen the discrepancies.

"Knock it off. Can't change, it. Move on," I said sternly.
These were orders I gave myself fairly often over the next few
weeks. It was good advice, but I just didn't seem to be able to
make it so.

Two months went by, where I ate excessive amounts of
cake and pouted and talked to my cats Jem and Scout. They
were sick of me. I was sick of me. The firm had promised that
my suspension was temporary. Didn't matter. I wouldn't go
back there now if they begged me. Which, of course, they'd
never do.

Time to throw in the towel, cut my losses. I needed a new
plan before I went bankrupt, too. My very, very last resort was to
call my parents. They would've helped me out, of course. I was
their only child, after all. But the price was more than I wanted
to pay. And despite the dire circumstances, I wasn't totally at the
end of my rope yet.

Instead, I called my best friend Ginny Park, and the wheels
were set in motion.

Before I gave up my rented apartment in California, I sent a
letter to Miss Charlotte. I couldn't simply leave the state and not
tell Miss Charlotte where I was going and why—it was different
with her than it was with my parents, on so many levels. I'd have
called her, but speaking the words aloud would disappoint her
beyond my ability to accept. I was brave, but not that brave.

After several drafts, I finally gave up trying to find the right
words to say and scribbled the facts on my last piece of
stationery, without mentioning my parents, because I already
knew Miss Charlotte wouldn't approve of me not telling them.

Dear Miss Charlotte,

So, this is will probably come as a huge surprise to you—it did to me—but I'm moving. Back to Michigan. Frontenac Island to be exact. I'll be working and living in the Park Hotel with Ginny Park's family. You remember Ginny? She was my best friend in college. We did everything together. I went to her family house for all the holidays. They are good people, and I'm relieved they are taking me in. Of course, my cats Jem and Scout will go with me. I couldn't possibly leave them.

You're probably wondering why I'm moving.

Well, I've been suspended from the practice of law. No fault of my own, mind you. My boss embezzled money from our clients. Stupid idiot. Of course, he got caught. And he never once thought about how it would affect me. Oh, I could strangle him. And I will if I ever see him again.

So, despite the fact I had nothing to do with it, that he acted on his own and I had no knowledge of his criminal actions, the firm, naturally, blamed me, too. They said they were investigating and would probably clear me, but I have my doubts. So I figured the best course of action was to be proactive and move on.

Now, I know you're thinking, why didn't I call you? Because I know you'd open your arms wide and invite me in. I couldn't let you do that, Miss Charlotte. You have done so much for me over the years, been there for me when my parents couldn't care less, and I know you have your hands full with your nephews. They need your wise, level-headed counsel. You took care of me for eighteen years like I was your own. You raised me to be strong and independent, and I don't want to fail you now by running to you with my tail between my legs. I won't. You taught me better than that.

Once I'm settled at the Park Hotel, I'll let you know how to reach me. Not sure how long I'll be there, but I feel like that's where I'm being led. Maybe you'll be able to come for a vacation. I would love to see you.

All my love,

Andi

And that's how I'd ended up at the Park Hotel, working as a concierge. Where I found the dead body.

CHAPTER TWO

GINNY PARK AND I had been the best of friends since college. We spent every day together at the University of Michigan before I left for Stanford to study law. She knew everything about me, including my isolated childhood. How I was raised by Miss Charlotte, my African-American nanny. How I loved Miss Charlotte to pieces, even now. And I knew everything about Ginny, including that she never wanted to get married and have children, to the chagrin of her parents.

So, of course, Ginny was the one I turned to when my life went to hell. And she was the one who offered me the only port in a very stormy situation.

She came to pick me up at the airport to take me to my new home. She'd sent photos of a lovely room at the Park Hotel on touristy and historic Frontenac Island, which her family owned and operated. I'd loved the place all of my life. It seemed like a dream come true that I'd actually live there, even under these circumstances.

"Andi!" Ginny shouted when she saw me, and in seconds, she had enveloped me in her skinny arms and a cloud of vanilla sweetness. I inhaled her welcome, realizing how much I'd truly missed her.

She squeezed me once more, then pulled back to really look at me. Echoing my thoughts, she said, "God, I've missed you."

"Me, too."

"You're thinner."

I looked down at myself, thinking that I'd probably put on five pounds in the past month, all on my hips. That was one thing I realized during this ordeal—I was definitely an emotional eater. I knew the cashier at the Dairy Queen by her first name. Jada and I had started to become very close. I even knew her kids' names.

I countered with, "Well, you seem a lot taller, somehow."

Ginny pulled up her boot-cut jeans to reveal platform heels.

"How can you walk in those?"

"Very carefully." She laughed, then her gaze tracked down to the cheap running shoes on my feet. They definitely didn't enhance the pinstriped cotton pants and sheer blouse I was wearing.

"My heel broke when I ran to catch my flight. I bought these in Detroit," I shook my head. "It's been a long day."

Ginny swung an arm around me, guiding me to the only luggage carousel in the terminal. "Let's get your luggage and get you home."

Home. I liked the sound of that. I only hoped it would feel like that when I got there. The last time I truly felt at home anywhere was when Ginny invited me to her parents' place in Kalamazoo for the holidays back in college.

My parents, who lived in Hong Kong now, didn't celebrate our holidays here in the US. Except for my birthday. That did warrant a ten-minute phone call from my mother and usually consisted of the obligatory questions about my job, my eating habits, and if I was in any sort of long-term relationship. Which I wasn't. Yet another reason why she was forever disappointed in me. I could only imagine how she'd react to my temporary suspension from practicing law. So, of course, I simply didn't tell her.

I stood at the carousel as it just started to turn. I heard my fur babies long before I saw them when their cat carriers came around the conveyor belt. The airline wouldn't let me take them into the cabin with me, and I'd been nervous as hell about leaving them on their own for the long trip. Ginny beamed as she grabbed the carriers. "Oh my God, they're so cute."

I reached in and petted Scout then Jem, and was rewarded with twin purrs. I smiled. They'd weathered the three flights just fine. Like me, they had indomitable spirits. I hoped they would be comfortable in their new home. If not, we'd have to move.

During the car ride to Frontenac City where we would catch the ferry over to the island, Ginny talked nonstop. I loved that about her, actually. There was never a lull where I felt required to jump in with something mundane or irrelevant. Ginny could always carry the conversational ball.

Although I already knew the basic story, she filled me in on her parents' move to the island five years ago to run the hotel after Ginny's granddad finally retired. It was a family affair. Ginny was the event organizer. Her brother Eric was the accountant, and his wife Nicole ran the restaurant.

I wondered what it would be like to see Eric again. We'd had a bit of a fling when I was in school with Ginny. After I realized he had a crush on me, we went on a couple of dates, but it didn't amount to much. He just wasn't my type, but Ginny told me later that I had hurt him deeply. This made things awkward for him and for me, but it was all water under the bridge. I hoped.

I grabbed Ginny's hand as she talked about the hotel, seeing she was starting to choke up a little. Her dad, Henry, had died three years ago, and I knew they'd been close. Actually, the whole family was close, something that I had always envied greatly.

My parents had literally never been there for me, and I didn't have any siblings. Ginny was basically the sister I'd never had; her parents the funny uncle and warm aunt I'd never experienced. I still kicked myself regularly for not coming to Henry's funeral because the firm wouldn't give me the time off.

"Are you sure your mom's okay with me coming to stay?"

"Oh God, yes. She loves you. She's always talked about how accomplished you are. She's very proud of you. I think she loves you more than me." Ginny laughed, but I could see something troubling in her expression.

"That can't be true. You're the perfect daughter."

"I'm just kidding around. I mean, she's not your mother, right?" Ginny's smile wavered a bit too much.

"Exactly right. According to my mother, I'm far, far from perfect." I squeezed her hand. "You're an absolute gem, you know that, right?"

"I know." She gave me her goofy Ginny grin that I missed so much. "You're going to love it, Andi. I promise you that. Lots of places you'll want to explore, the way you loooooooove to do. Tons of stuff going on all the time. You'll never want to leave."

I returned her smile, then looked out the window as we neared the ferry station. I loved the water. It was one of the reasons I had stayed in California, so I could enjoy the ocean whenever I had the time. Which unfortunately did not turn out to be as much as I had hoped, but still it was there if I ever needed to see it.

Lake Michigan wasn't the Pacific Ocean, but from the shore, it could've easily passed because it was so huge. The lake had waves, too. Not as rolling or large as the ocean, but still present with the driving force of the wind. The smell was a bit different, too. Ocean air smelled and tasted salty—not so with the Great Lakes. The aroma was fresher, cleaner, like it had been washed by rain moments ago. I rolled down my window and inhaled it all in.

Then we were driving into the ferry's reserved parking lot for the twenty-five-minute ride across the water to the island. Ginny chatted with Peggy, the girl at the ferry station ticket booth, and introduced us when she bought my season pass that would allow me unlimited trips for the summer.

If I wasn't excited before, I was now. We walked onto the ferry and went to sit on the top deck. The ferry was full to capacity, but most of the tourists sat below, out of the wind, watching the approach to the grand old place.

The green of the island was the first thing I noticed. There were trees everywhere. Next was the bay we were docking into. The water was so clear and blue, and the beach sand was actually soft in some areas. The beaches around most of the island were rocky. Maybe they had sand shipped in for swimmers hardy enough to brave the icy water. This was a tourist destination after all.

But what took my breath away was the huge Park Hotel perched on the cliff side. It was a colonial style, three stories with white clapboard siding and round pillars and a cupola on top that housed a charming old-fashioned bar with spectacular views. Even from the water, I could see the colorful umbrellas dotting the massive garden that spread out from the hotel to the cliff. The sight was breathtaking.

Ginny nudged me in the side. "What do you think?"

"I think I'm going to love my new home."

CHAPTER THREE

ONCE WE WERE TIED up, Ginny and I walked off the ferry,
each with a cat carrier in hand. She waved to the two old guys
sitting at a table on the dock playing a game of chess.

"That's JC and Reggie," she said of the two grizzled men.
"They're permanent fixtures down here. But if you are ever in
need of information about the island, they'll give you the
lowdown and then some." She laughed. "Sometimes they're in
disagreement about the accuracy of the lowdown, but you'll be
wiser for it anyway."

I waved to JC and Reggie, just to be friendly. Main Street
was filled with locals and tourists riding bicycles and horse-
drawn carriages. I sneezed. Twice. The aroma of horse droppings
in the street was pungent, not to mention the actual traveling
hazards presented.

"You'll get used to it," Ginny grinned. "I'm sorry the Park's
carriage couldn't pick us up, but we're just too busy this
weekend. One of the guys will collect your luggage later. But

we'll need to walk up the hill to the hotel. Are you good with that?"

I nodded and shifted Jem's carrier to my other hand. "I could use the exercise. But Jem and Scout will get pretty heavy."

"That's okay. We can stop to rest. It's not that far, and we're in no hurry." Ginny transferred Scout's crate to her other side, and we were off to the Park Hotel.

The walk to the hotel was about half a mile, mostly uphill along a winding road lit by old-style streetlamps. Ginny led the way around to the back where the employees' entrances were, and we went inside.

The color scheme was the first thing that hit me. It was all papered walls, green velvet chairs and sofas, and red floral carpeting. Technically it should've been a disgusting color combination, but it actually really worked well together, giving the place a rich, vibrant, historical vibe.

"Welcome to the Park Hotel." Ginny did a twirl with her arms out. "What do you think?"

"It's beautiful."

"Right? I couldn't believe it when Mom and Dad decided to buy the place with Grandpa Sam. Like, honestly, I don't know how they did it. It wasn't like we're rich or anything. I think maybe Grandpa fronted them most of the cash."

I looked around, taking it all in, just as Lois Park, Ginny's mother, came around the corner with her arms open wide to greet me.

"Andi!" She hugged me tightly. Lois always gave the best hugs. "I'm so happy you're here."

"Me, too," I said, meaning it with my entire soul.

Then her gaze flitted over the cat carriers. Scout and Jem were meowing loudly. They hadn't eaten in quite a while, so they were both hungry and letting us know about it. "What are those?"

"My cats."

She tapped a finger to her mouth. "I'm afraid you're not going to be able to keep them here."

My heart sank. I'd come so far. And there was no way I would give up my cats. Jem and Scout were much too dear. Most days, they felt like the only family I had. "I'm sorry. I didn't know."

Ginny grabbed her mother's arm. "I'm sure we can make an exception for Andi."

"You can keep them here for a few days until you can make arrangements, but we can't have pets in the hotel. A rule you are well aware of, Ginny."

"It'll be fine." Ginny grabbed my hand. "I actually know a great person who can take care of them for you. Her name is Daisy, and she runs a kennel and grooming place. She's great."

Lois frowned. "Mmm. Are you sure about her? She's a bit flighty, don't you think?"

My face must've given away my emotions, because Ginny squeezed my hand harder. I glanced at my darlings and couldn't imagine my life without them. Maybe this whole plan, this whole move was not a good idea. I would never have made the leap if I'd known Scout and Jem weren't welcome. But then we'd all be sleeping in a cardboard box under the freeway, probably.

"Mom, you think everyone is flighty. You think I'm flighty."

Lois pursed her lips. "Yeah, well…"

Before she could finish, Ginny pulled me away. "C'mon, I'll show you your room."

"We'll talk later," Lois said to me in a tone that was more like a promised appointment with doom than a pleasant invitation.

Ginny led me past the huge lobby, which had chandeliers hanging from a domed ceiling and black and white tiles on the floor. Everything was bright and polished and extravagant. The Park Hotel felt like a historic palace. I knew I'd love it here, just like Ginny promised.

She turned the corner and took us to the far side of the hotel where she and the family had their suites overlooking Lake Michigan and the Frontenac Bridge that connected the state's upper and lower peninsulas. The views were stunning.

"Here's you." She stopped in front of suite 108.

"I'm down that hall," she pointed, "and Eric is down the opposite way with Nicole. Mom has a separate cottage on the west bluff overlooking the water." She swiped the key card and opened the door for me. We shuffled in with cats in tow.

I was pleasantly surprised to see black and white tile at the entrance and pretty wallpaper with white and purple flowers everywhere.

Ginny smiled when she saw my expression. "It's called the Lilac Suite, and I thought it was perfect for you."

There was a small foyer with a closet and decorative table and mirror. Then we entered a cute living room, with a deep-purple velvet sofa and chair, and a glass coffee table with a beautiful decorative rug underneath.

To the immediate right was a kitchenette with a mini refrigerator, sink, counter, and some cupboards. A couple of feet over was a raised area with two steps that led to the queen-sized bed and dressers. And beyond the living room along one wall were just windows and a French door that opened up onto my own private patio facing the lake.

I felt like I'd landed in a fairy tale. Cinderella-like, almost. But without Prince Charming, thankfully. A prince would complicate my life way too much right at the moment.

"It's nice, right?" she asked, anxious for my approval.

I blinked away tears before I turned to my friend. "It's perfect. Thank you, Ginny."

She opened the cat carriers and proceeded to pick up Scout and rub her little black head. "And don't worry about these guys. I'll talk to Mom. I'll convince her they won't be a problem."

Jem must've liked that idea, because he immediately started to purr and rub against Ginny's legs. He was basically a little flirt. He was tan and beautifully marked almost like a Savannah, which made him irresistible, of course.

I walked to the windows and smiled. The tension in my shoulders and neck released a little. Everything was going to be okay. My life was just experiencing a little hiccup, a tiny setback. And this was not a bad place to ride it through. I had my best friend, my fur babies, the tenacity to not let anything get me down, and a perfect little piece of paradise to call my home. What could possibly go wrong?

CHAPTER FOUR

FOR THE NEXT COUPLE of days, as Ginny instructed, I familiarized myself with the hotel and the grounds. I took all my meals in the restaurant, where the food was top-notch. I swam in the pool—the water heated to a perfect temperature—and I indulged in a massage and pedicure in the spa, which was both relaxing and a special treat for myself. I walked through the gardens and attempted the hedge maze. I got lost twice, and that was fun, too.

This was all good research as it so happened, because Ginny had announced the next day that she'd found me a job. As concierge in the hotel no less, since the current one, Casey, had to take a leave of absence to care for his mother who just had hip surgery. I didn't know anything about being a concierge, but it was the best she could do for me job-wise, and I needed the money. I was on my last few hundred dollars, and some of that had to go to my credit card bill to pay for those plane tickets that got me out here. I was way too old and too proud to be asking my parents for a loan, and I definitely wouldn't want to deal with whatever strings they'd attach to the money, anyway.

Early Friday morning, I showed up in the lobby in a pair of black pinstriped pants and a black-and-white floral silk top, ready to learn just what I had signed up for. I'd stayed at several top rated hotels over the years and had dealt with the concierges to book taxis and tickets to the hottest attractions. I could do this. I was good with people, and I was a stellar negotiator, so I knew I could get the best deals and best prices for the guests.

What I didn't expect was to get thrown into a war zone on my first day.

The hotel was abuzz with activity even at five a.m. as cleaners and hotel staff prepared for the annual chamber of commerce convention. Something that Ginny had failed to mention when she told me my first day would be on Friday— even though she was the event organizer at the hotel and it should have been top on her mind. My flighty friend. There was going to be four days of meetings and lunches, suppers and drinks in the garden. And as it turned out, I was expected to help set it all up.

Before I could get out a friendly "Good morning," Lois marched toward me with a clipboard. "I need you to call June and make sure she's going to be here with the flowers on time."

I took the clipboard she'd thrust at me. "Who's June, and where's her number?"

"June Biddle. June's Blooms, our florist. Her number is on the computer on the concierge desk over there. Where you'll be working." She pointed to the round, white wooden desk located near the main doors that said CONCIERGE on it in gold letters.

I marched over to the desk and clicked on the computer, determined to prove myself to Lois. She wasn't as convinced as Ginny that I was a good fit for the job. Honestly, I think it had more to do with the fact that Lois didn't value her daughter's opinion than it was about me being unqualified. To my way of thinking, it didn't take a Rhodes Scholar to be a concierge at a tourist hotel on an island as small as Frontenac. I'd handled much tougher assignments when I was a lawyer, for sure.

Eric had actually laughed when Ginny told him what she had in mind for me. His laugh seemed a bit forced. Our first meeting after so many years didn't go well. It was more than a bit awkward, and his wife Nicole gave me the stink eye the entire time we talked. Obviously, Eric must've told her some unflattering stuff about me. I didn't know what it could be. In my mind, we had parted as friends. But I guess not.

After a few frustrating clicks on the mouse, I figured out where the business contact list was stored, located June Biddle's phone number, and called it. She answered almost immediately. I introduced myself, explained what I needed, and she agreed to provide it. Piece of cake. I'd completed my first assignment without a hitch.

After a few more successful calls to various businesses, making sure everything was set for the weekend, I was feeling pretty good about myself. At least until the guests started showing up for the chamber of commerce meeting, demanding things that I had no clue about.

The first wounding shot had come from the town mayor, Lindsey Hamilton.

She marched up to the desk in a stylish pewter-blue pantsuit with a simple black scoop-neck top under it, which I loved and would've asked where she'd bought if she wasn't blowing smoke out her nostrils like an angry bull. "The water in the pitchers in the conference rooms is tepid. The water should be cold."

"Okay, I'm sorry to hear that, and I'll just call—"

"Get it changed now. People are starting to arrive, and they'll want cold water."

"Ma'am, if you—"

Her eyes bugged out. "Ma'am? Do you not know who I am?"

I didn't. Not then. "I'm sorry if I've offended you, but this is my first—"

Ginny came rushing across the lobby. "Mayor Hamilton, how can I help?"

"Oh, Virginia, thank God. I was just telling this…person about the problem in the conference room."

Ginny put her hand on the mayor's shoulder. "I will fix whatever needs to be fixed. It's my fault that Andi wasn't prepped to handle any hiccups that might occur with the conference. That is completely on me."

Mayor Hamilton turned to glance at me, and I smiled at her. I could see she was stressed out.

"I'm sorry," she said.

I shook my head and smiled. "No need to apologize, Mayor Hamilton. I'm brand spanking new to all of this, kinda winging it until I learn all the ropes. Thank you for understanding."

She returned my smile, but her heart wasn't in it. Ginny gave me the thumbs-up behind her back. Then she ushered the mayor back to the conference rooms where Ginny would put out the fires with that fresh cold water.

The rest of the morning and early afternoon I was swamped with directing all the business people to the conference rooms, organizing horse-drawn taxis, luggage storage, making restaurant reservations for groups of two and three and ten.

Not only was it the chamber of commerce convention, but the first June weekend of the busy season. Tourists flocked to the island and the historic Park Hotel. Turned out, this was both the best and the worst weekend to make my debut as concierge. I enjoyed learning and being busy, and I was normally solid under huge amounts of stress. But handling the volume of guest demands gave new meaning to the phrase "under pressure."

At around two, there was a slight lull. Enough that I was able to run to the Lady Slipper Tea Room, which was on the main floor of the hotel, to grab a ham-and-swiss panini and a bottle of strawberry-infused Kombucha tea. I had to start eating better if I was going to survive this job.

After paying for my food, I twisted the lid on the bottle, took a sip, and turned to head back to my desk. Which was when I literally ran into five-foot-ten of lean muscle mass in a cobalt-blue suit. The Kombucha spilled over the rim of the bottle and splashed over a pair of shiny black shoes. I looked down at the shoes then quickly up into a chiseled face with startling light-blue eyes.

"Whoops," was what came out of my mouth.

He gave me a look that said, *Are you kidding me?* Then he reached for the napkins in the dispenser on the counter and crouched to wipe off his shoes.

I cringed. "Sorry about that."

"It's fine. I was probably standing too close behind you."

"Yeah, I was wondering whose breath that was on my neck," I said with a laugh.

He didn't share my attempt to lighten the mood, just continued to wipe at his still shiny shoes.

I took my panini and scurried back to the concierge desk, thinking the day couldn't get any worse. But of course, I was dead wrong on that count.

CHAPTER FIVE

THE WORST REALLY STARTED in the form of an obese man in a floral shirt, wet swim trunks, and flip-flops. He smelled like chlorine. His sweaty bald head was almost hypnotizing in the bright light streaming in through the big plate-glass windows. I had to concentrate on looking at his face.

"I lost my wallet."

"Okay. Where did you see it last?"

"I don't know."

I smiled. "Did you have it this morning when you woke up?"

"Yes. It was on the table."

"Here, in your room at the hotel?"

He nodded.

"Okay, so did you check your room?"

"Yup, and it wasn't there."

"Did you go to the restaurant for breakfast? Did you have it with you then?"

"Nope, we ordered room service."

"I see. Did you go out anywhere this morning?"

He screwed up his face as he did some serious thinking. Before he could answer me, though, his wife and four kids came shrieking across the lobby. There was no other way of describing it. His kids were literally shrieking like the wraiths from *Lord of the Rings*.

"Did you find it yet?" his wife demanded.

He shook his head, and sweat drops landed on the desk. Luckily I'd moved my hands just in time. "This lady is trying to help me find it."

The woman gave me a look. "It doesn't look like she's trying very hard."

I wanted to slap her, honestly, but instead I ignored her and said to the man, "How about you write down your name here and your room number." I set a piece of paper and a pen on the counter in front of him. "I'll inform the cleaning staff and the front desk to be on the lookout for your wallet."

The woman sniffed and said loudly, "They'll probably steal everything in it before handing it in."

Other guests had now turned to look at us. The last thing I needed was a complaint about me and how I mishandled things.

"I assure you that I will go look for your wallet, personally."

The man wrote down his name, *Herb Lowry*, his room number, *306*, and smiled at me. "Oh, you know, I remember now that I went for a swim this morning."

Then he went off with his wife nattering at him and his four kids pulling at his ugly floral shirt, trying to get his attention. Poor guy. I'd probably lose more than my wallet if I had to deal with that crew on a daily basis.

When the lobby emptied after the dinner rush, I called the front desk and told Lane, one of the front desk clerks, that I was just stepping away for a few minutes. I headed for the pool. Most likely Herb had left his wallet on one of the lounge chairs before he went swimming and totally forgot about it.

As I neared the end of the corridor, I noticed that a CLOSED FOR CLEANING sign was in front of the entrance to the pool area. Maintenance hadn't informed the front desk or me that they'd be closing the pool, but maybe that wasn't how things worked around here. I was still learning the ropes. I would ask about that later.

I swiped my employee card and opened the door, nearly slipping on the water on the threshold. The dampness in the air hit me immediately. My mascara was probably going to run down my face. I lifted my arms to air out my armpits. My blouse would probably end up sticking to me by the time I did the rounds and got out of there. Thankfully, the pool was empty of swimmers, so I didn't have to be concerned about getting splashed by errant chlorinated water. I didn't want to smell like Herb for the rest of the night.

Walking around the pool, I checked all the loungers—there were at least twenty—and then struck gold when I spotted something dark and square on the floor near the corner.

Herb's wallet was sitting all by itself near one of the planters. I wondered if someone had found it, riffled through it, and then tossed it. I really hoped not. I didn't want Mrs. Herb Lowry accusing me of stealing his money or credit cards. I opened the wallet just in case. Two hundred cash in the billfold and three credit cards in place. Maybe that was everything. I crossed my fingers. At least I'd found it. That was a win, right?

Clutching the wallet like a first-place trophy, I turned to leave and nearly slipped again. There was a lot of water on the pool deck. Surprising, since the CLOSED sign meant the cleaning had already been done or was in process, although I didn't see any staff or any equipment laid out for that job.

I'd have to call the maintenance staff and get the water cleaned up. I expected some pool water on the surround. People sloshed around as they got in and out of the pool. But it just seemed excessive to me, especially this far from the pool's edge.

While looking down at the wet tiles, I spotted something dark along some of the grout. Looked like rust. I'd let Ginny know. Lois definitely wouldn't approve. Someone should have a word with the cleaning staff to make sure that whatever it was got cleaned up before Lois found out about it.

My gaze followed the trail of rust and water, and it led to the maintenance room. Maybe it was some kind of chemical leaking, which was not a good thing at all. I'd check things out before I reported to Ginny. We might need more than the cleaning crew down here. And the hotel certainly didn't need the pool out of service for the busy weekend.

I knew it was possible the door might be locked, but I gave it a try anyway. Nope, not locked.

It was dark inside, and I fumbled along the wall near the door for the light switch. I flicked it, and ugly yellow fluorescent light flooded the small room.

My gaze followed the line of rusty liquid along the floor, which appeared darker and redder the farther away from the pool it went.

That's when I spotted the source of the rusty liquid.

Except it wasn't rust.

It was blood.

And it was leaking from a body, pale and greasy, shoved into a utility closet between the mop and the water vacuum like just another pool accessory.

CHAPTER SIX

IT TOOK A FEW minutes before I could breathe again and got my pounding heart under control. I sprang into action.

After I made sure that he was actually dead—he was—I tamped down the bile rising in my throat and called Ginny, told her she needed to come to the pool ASAP. Before she could probe me further, I called Lois and advised her of the same thing. Lois must've called Eric, because all of three them rushed through the door around the same time.

"What is going on?" Lois demanded.

I pointed to the maintenance room. "There's a dead body stuffed in the closet."

My voice, even to my ears, sounded level and cold, but inside I was vibrating with shock.

All three of them frowned at me. Then Ginny let out a giggle. "She's just having us on. Not the best time to be joking around, Andi."

I just looked at her. "I would never just joke around about something like that."

Her grin faded. "That's true."

Lois and Eric went to peek into the room.

"Oh good Lord," Eric turned right back around, his face instantly pale. He bent over and took in some deep breaths. It looked like he was going to vomit.

Lois just shook her head. "Henry's not going to be happy about this."

"Daddy's dead, Mom. I don't think he's going to care," Ginny said, scowling.

Lois waved her hand at her daughter. "Force of habit."

After that, there had been a lot of hand flapping and gasping by Ginny and Eric as I explained how I came across the body. Lois, on the other hand, was pretty stoic about the whole thing. She made sure the pool's entry was locked, had a POOL IS TEMPORARILY CLOSED sign posted in the lobby, and informed the front reception staff of the situation. She calmed both her children and told them to plant their butts in chairs to wait for the sheriff, whom she called. I was impressed. Lois seemed unflappable.

As for me, I'd seen a dead body before. I was there when my grandmother died, but it was peacefully in her bed surrounded by friends and hospice staff. Not like this. This was not peaceful, and it definitely wasn't a natural death. The man had a nasty gash in his forehead. That's where the blood came from. Someone had hit him with something heavy, and I knew the poor guy hadn't stuffed himself into the utility closet. This was no accident. The man was obviously murdered.

My hands were still shaking by the time Sheriff Luke Jackson joined Ginny, Lois, Eric, and me.

While one deputy snapped pictures of the crime scene and the body, the sheriff asked me to go over the course of events that led to my grisly discovery. As I talked, my lawyer experience kicked in, and I made sure to give him an exact timeline. I knew how important it was. He made his notes and then asked me more questions.

"Had you seen the deceased before?"

"No. Not that I recall."

"And you were at the concierge desk the entire day?"

"Yes, but it has been very busy today with the meetings and weekend arrivals. And it's my first day on the job."

His brow furrowed as he tapped his pen against his notebook. I was pretty sure the sheriff was in his early forties— Ginny had mentioned it to me while we were waiting, as well as the fact that he was divorced and looking for a girlfriend. (I couldn't believe Ginny was already trying to set me up with someone, especially now.) The lines on his face made me think he'd already had a pretty hard life. He had nice eyes, though, and a strong jaw. The right woman would come along for him. But that woman wasn't me.

Ginny told me this was the first murder they'd had since she'd been living at the Park Hotel. There was some famous unsolved one from decades ago, but that was it. Murder was not something that usually happened on Frontenac Island.

The deputy, Marshall was his name, came up to the sheriff's side. He handed him a black wallet. "Found it in his back pants pocket."

"Anything else on him?"

The deputy shook his head.

"Okay, go out front and wait for the coroner. He should be coming from the mainland."

"Shouldn't he take pictures of the pool and the deck?" I blurted before I could stop myself.

The sheriff raised an angry eyebrow. "Excuse me?"

"The whole area is a crime scene, isn't it?"

"Yes," he snapped. "Why?"

"I mean, the murder weapon could be anywhere. Blunt force trauma to the head doesn't just happen. There could be hair and fibers and fingerprints," I said.

"We're aware," he said sternly.

"Also, he had to have a hotel key card on him or else he wouldn't have been able to get in here. It's locked to those who aren't guests of the hotel or actual hotel staff."

"Good to know. Thank you," he replied, but he sounded more angry than grateful.

"Unless the killer let him in, then in that case, the killer would have a hotel key card." My mind was spinning with details. So much to do.

The deputy glanced at the sheriff, then back at me, his eyes wide and unsure.

Sheriff Jackson narrowed his gaze at me, probably pissed off that I'd pointed out the obvious stuff he and the deputy should have known.

"Take pictures of the entire area and then go wait for the coroner," he finally said to the deputy.

The deputy nodded.

"Miss..." the sheriff glanced down at his notebook, "...Steele, I don't know how things are done where you're from—"

"Most recently, California," I interceded.

"Uh-huh. But here, I'm in charge."

"Well—"

Lois stepped up, putting a hand on my shoulder, effectively
shutting me down. "Sheriff, whatever you need, you just ask.
Everyone at the hotel is at *your* disposal."

He sucked on his teeth and glared at me. "Uh-huh." He
opened the wallet and fished out the dead man's ID. "Thomas
Banks. Name sound familiar?"

"No, not offhand," Lois said.

I shook my head. "We can check—" There was that hand on
my shoulder again.

"I will make sure we examine the registry to see if he was a
guest of the hotel," Lois said.

He nodded. "I'll need to question the hotel staff."

"Of course," Lois said.

With a nod of his head to Lois, and definitely not to me, he
moved over to speak with Ginny and Eric.

Lois gave me a very boss-like look. "What are you doing?"

"Cooperating with the police."

"You were trying to tell that man how to do his job."

"I'm a lawyer."

"Not anymore, you're not, Andi. You're the concierge at my
hotel."

She didn't need to add "at my discretion." It was completely
implied by her tone of voice. She knew that I knew she could
easily take my job away. Sure, we had history, and she'd treated
me like a daughter in the past, but I wasn't her daughter. I was
just a friend Ginny wanted to help out. I needed to be careful if I
wanted to stay.

"You're right. I'm sorry. I won't get in the way of the
sheriff's investigation."

"Good." She patted my shoulder, then softened. "Are you
okay? I imagine it was quite a shock to find…" She waved her

hand in the direction of the maintenance room where another young deputy was standing by the open door. His face was green.

"I'm fine."

She looked me over then nodded. "Yeah, you were always made of stern stuff. Not like my Ginny."

We both glanced over at Ginny as she spoke to the sheriff. She was sniffling while tears ran down her cheeks. She'd always been sensitive. But I had to admit, I honestly loved that about her. She was just so free and easy with her emotions.

So different from me.

Eric once told me that I was one of the most guarded women he'd ever known. I knew when he said that he really meant "cold." I was pretty sure I came by that honestly from my parents. My mother, in particular, was the iciest person ever to walk the earth. I swore she was solely responsible for the fact that seventy percent of the earth's fresh water was frozen. She was the real Snow Queen.

Lois said, "Come with me to talk to the mayor and the rest of our guests at the chamber of commerce meeting. We need to explain what's going on."

I nodded, and away we went.

CHAPTER SEVEN

FORTY-FIVE MINUTES LATER, I was standing with Lois Park, Mayor Hamilton, and the sheriff just outside the conference room to go over the situation. We hadn't told the guests anything, but we'd informed the staff.

After conferring with the front desk, we discovered that the victim, Thomas Banks, had checked into the hotel this morning and was booked into room 209. Lane, who had checked him in, said that Thomas claimed he was here on business. But there was no Thomas Banks registered for the chamber of commerce meetings. When asked, Mayor Hamilton said she didn't recognize the name.

"Do we need to cancel the conference?" the mayor asked. "I would hope not. A lot of planning has gone into this, and there are lots of good businesses represented. The island economy needs this, too."

"I don't think canceling will be necessary for the time being," the sheriff said.

I was about to offer my opinion on the matter, when tall-and-handsome from the tea room strode toward us. He was wearing a different suit and shoes. I really hoped my tea hadn't been the reason for that. "I heard there was a murder," he said.

The mayor nodded. "This is Mayor Daniel Evans from Frontenac City on the mainland." Sheriff Jackson shook his hand.

"Daniel, this is Lois Park, the hotel proprietor. And this is…" She frowned at me. "I'm sorry. I don't know your name or why you are here."

"I'm Andi Steele…"

Lois interjected, "She's our concierge and needs to be apprised of the situation to better serve our guests. She's also the one who found Mr. Banks."

Mayor Evans nodded toward me, likely recognizing me as the dolt who spilled tea all over his expensive shoes. "What's the course of action here?"

"I was just explaining to the sheriff how I felt it would be a real loss to the island if we had to cancel our conference," Mayor Hamilton said.

"I agree," Mayor Evans said, "but there must be a proper procedure we need to follow. A man has been killed."

I nodded. "If I may—"

"Andi," Lois warned, "what did we discuss?"

"I know, it's just…well, if I were in charge, I would close the hotel and prevent anyone from leaving and anyone new from checking in." The sheriff's frown really deepened, but I kept going since I was already on a roll. No point in stopping now. "I mean, as far as we know, the killer has already left the hotel. And if he hasn't, he will soon. Everyone will need to be sequestered inside until they all can be questioned and their whereabouts verified for the time of the murder."

Lois sighed and shook her head.

Mayor Hamilton cocked her hip and arched one of her sculpted eyebrows. "That would take several hours. Daniel and I have reservations in the village at the Seaside Grill for a late dinner and drinks with the biggest land developer in Michigan. Several other business owners from the island and from the mainland will be joining us. We can't possibly miss it."

"Yes, but wouldn't you say solving this murder is more important?" I countered.

No one looked amused. Although Mayor Evans looked like maybe he wanted to smile. It could've been wishful thinking on my part. I'd yet to see him smile, but I'd have bet he could flash a megawatter when he wanted to.

Sheriff Jackson grabbed my arm and pulled me to the side. "We need to have a conversation."

"Fine." I pulled my arm out of his grip. "But I don't like to be manhandled."

He rubbed a hand over his face. "I apologize." He didn't sound even a little bit sorry.

"Look, Sheriff, I'm not trying to tell you how to do your job, but you have to admit I'm right. You know you need to preserve the integrity of the scene. Evidence of all kinds is already lost at this point, wouldn't you say?" I paused. "The killer's lawyer will have a field day if you fail to follow procedures here. You don't want the killer to get away scot-free, do you?"

Sheriff Jackson scowled. "Ms. Steele, I heard you were some hotshot lawyer out west, and that's fine. But here, I'm the law. I'm in charge. What I say goes."

"Then *be* in charge…because all I've seen so far—"

"Don't finish that sentence, Ms. Steele. I don't want to have to take you down to the station and interrogate you for the rest of night."

"On what grounds?"

"On the grounds that you're pissing me off."

"Sheriff—"

He put up his hand to stop my next words. "I will make sure no one leaves and that we question everyone."

I grinned. I couldn't keep the smugness out of it, though.

"I've got two deputies here right now, and two others I could call in to help."

"I could help," I offered. "I have extensive experience with witness interviews."

"No. Absolutely not."

"Sheriff, I could be invaluable to you."

He rubbed a hand over his face again and gave me a hard stare. "Ms. Steele, the last thing you will ever be to me is invaluable. The best thing for you to do is to help Lois organize the rooms where my deputies can question people. Other than that, please stay out of my way."

He strode back to where the others stood and explained his plan. Which was really my plan, although he didn't give me any credit for it. But I would do what he asked and stay out of his way.

Or at least I would give it the old college try.

Oh, who was I kidding? I wasn't going to stay out of it.

I was smack-dab in the middle of it, and I was going to find out who killed Thomas Banks. I couldn't do anything about my old boss stealing millions from clients and costing me my job, but this I could do. And I would.

CHAPTER EIGHT

BY THE TIME THE sheriff and his deputies finished all the interviews, it was well past midnight, and there were a lot of tired, angry hotel guests. I tried to ease the suffering, since in a way it was my fault that everyone was held for questioning in various conference rooms. I made sure there were plenty of drinks and food, courtesy of the hotel, which perturbed Lois, but I figured it was the responsible thing to do, considering the situation.

I was able to placate the mayors, too, by suggesting we put them in a separate room with the business people they had planned to join for dinner and provide them with a meal and drinks. They could schmooze in between interviews.

The food was easy to manage—the hotel's head chef, Justin, just happened to be Mayor Hamilton's husband. So, thankfully, that was convenient. At least now when I entered the room, she didn't give me a death glare; it was more of an annoyed glance. I figured that was progress.

While I managed to stay out of Sheriff Jackson's way during the interviews, I did keep my ears and eyes open. I got a nugget of info, indirectly, from a very yappy deputy named Shawn (the green-faced deputy who was guarding the maintenance room earlier). He was trying to impress the group of bridesmaids at the hotel for a bachelorette party and told them the coroner put the time of death somewhere between two and seven p.m.

Since I discovered the body at around eight, and he had looked rather fresh and not stiff with rigor—yes, I had checked and lifted his arm—TOD was likely closer to seven than two. Which then frightened me a bit to think that if I had entered the area any earlier, I could have run into the killer. I'd like to think I would've acted proactively. I'd taken several self-defense classes, so I would've been prepared, but a person never knows how they are going to react in a life-or-death situation until it's upon them. Frankly, I didn't want to test that theory.

After the sheriff gave the go-ahead to release everyone, I helped Lois and Ginny get the guests back to their rooms or to horse-drawn taxis if they were leaving the hotel.

The staff members were none too happy with me once they found out I'd been the one to make the interview suggestion. There were a lot of grumblings about not being paid overtime to stick around and answer questions. How they found out it was my suggestion remained a mystery, but my money was on Eric's wife. Nicole managed the restaurant and the waitstaff. She seemed to have all kinds of animosity toward me. As if it was my fault poor Mr. Banks was murdered and stuffed inside the pool's utility closet.

While assisting the guests after the interviews, I ran into Herb Lowry and his wife. He'd thanked me for finding his wallet and apologized profusely that searching for it had been the reason I had found the body.

How everyone knew I'd found the body perplexed me, too. Who the heck would be spreading that around? I would've thought the sheriff would want that piece of information kept confidential.

I suppose it was the curse of small towns and me being the outsider. They all knew each other, and no one knew much about me. I'd been on the job for less than twenty-four hours.

Gossip tended to spread quickly and efficiently under such circumstances. I hoped that would aid me in my quest to find the killer. If not, it should make the sheriff's job easier. Or possibly more complicated. Gossip worked two ways: it could shed light on a situation, or it could really muddle things.

While Herb Lowry was all apologetic, his wife was straight-up opportunistic. She hounded me for the next twenty minutes about how the hotel should pay for their four-day stay. That it was only fair, considering the undue stress it had put on her and their children. Children who had been happily entertained for the past five hours free of charge by hotel staff who plied them with snacks and drinks and a movie at the small on-site theatre.

I told her the best I could do was a free gift basket from the local soap company. She seemed to be happy with that, miraculously. For the moment, anyway.

CHAPTER NINE

AFTER EVERYONE WAS SECURED in their rooms, I was able to drag my butt back to my suite. I'd worked many long days for the firm in the past, but this day had been exhausting. Almost twenty-four hours of non-stop problems and not much food or water.

My body was still a bit shaky. Probably one part dehydration, one part shock. I needed sustenance. Since the hotel convenience store was closed, I figured I'd just pop by one of the vending machines. So what if the only one in the whole place just happened to be by the pool and spa? It was pure coincidence. I mean, it was on the way to my suite. Sort of. If I happened to do a roundabout first. And then ventured down a dead-end corridor.

The area was cordoned off, not by police tape—that would've been too unseemly to satisfy Lois Park's customer service standards—but by the big sign that read CLOSED DUE TO CLEANING.

I'd asked about that sign earlier. Maintenance staff claimed they had not in fact shut the pool area down to clean it. Which probably meant the sign was put there by the killer.

I couldn't risk entering the enclosure; the sheriff would be livid and probably charge me with something like obstruction of justice, so I just looked around the corridor. There was only one way in and out of the hallway leading to the pool and spa.

Looking up, I searched for closed circuit cameras. There were none, but I did spy the door to the stairwell. I went over and opened the door, which did not need a key card, and saw it led up to the guest rooms.

Back to the pool doors, my gaze swept over the floor and walls.

I wasn't sure what I was looking for; it wasn't like I was just going to magically stumble upon the murder weapon. But something just didn't sit right with me.

I looked down at the red carpet in front of the door to the pool's entrance. Had it been wet before I discovered the body?

I remembered almost slipping when I'd opened the door and gone inside. The floor had been excessively wet around the pool. The body had a lot of water around it, too.

Which meant it had been wet at some point.

Which probably meant it had been in the pool.

So, a strong possibility was that the victim had been hit in the head and fell into the pool.

That would mean the killer had to pull the body out of the pool, drag it to the utility room, and stuff it in the closet.

The killer would've been soaked during the process.

That meant he or she—I couldn't necessarily rule out a woman, although it required a lot of strength to drag that body—would have exited the pool area wet with soggy clothes.

A wet person in wet clothes would've been noticed walking around the hotel, so that didn't happen.

Adrenaline spiked inside me as I put the pieces together. My gaze landed on the frosted glass doors leading to the spa.

Since the spa closed at six, the doors would've been locked by the time the victim was killed, but that didn't necessarily mean no one got inside later. The spa would've been a good place to change out of wet clothes inconspicuously.

I cupped my hands on the glass and peered inside. Unfortunately, I couldn't see much from this vantage point. I needed to get in there.

I tried the door. It was locked. I needed a special key card, which I did not have with me, to open it. The killer wouldn't have had the special key card, either.

How would he get inside without breaking in through the front door? How would he get in without being seen?

Was there a back door?

"What are you doing?" Lois Park said sternly behind me.

I jumped a foot and banged my head into the glass. Rubbing my head, I turned to see Lois frowning at me from the mouth of the corridor. "Nothing."

"It's late. You should get some sleep. Tomorrow will be another busy day."

"You're right." I walked toward her.

She patted me on the shoulder. "It won't always be this crazy here. Eventually you'll get into a routine and be more comfortable dealing with the guests. I know it's hard filling such big shoes. Casey, our regular concierge, is very well loved here."

I nodded. "Yes, I've heard that." More than once actually. Many times. People kept saying it to me all day long. To the point that I'd wondered whether Casey was some kind of genius or if I was just that inadequate.

"Goodnight," Lois said.

"Night." I made my way down the corridor. I heard Lois's voice as I walked and thought she was talking to me, so I stopped and turned.

But she wasn't even looking at me. She was looking straight ahead at...no one. "I know, Henry. But for Ginny's sake, we should at least give her a chance."

My gut clenched at the sight of Lois talking to her dead husband, and I turned and kept walking, not wanting to disturb her. Was she delusional? Maybe. Or maybe Henry was really there, and I just couldn't see him. Old places like the Park Hotel were thought to be haunted sometimes. I would mention it to Ginny next time I saw her, just in case it was something to be concerned about—her mom talking to dead people.

I shook off the eerie feeling as I left the corridor and came out into the lobby. As I went to turn the corner to head to my suite, I spotted Frontenac City Mayor Daniel Evans going out the front doors. He was no longer wearing a business suit. Instead, he sported spandex running shorts and a t-shirt that hugged a very nicely toned body. *Not bad.*

When I finally reached my room, I opened the door and nearly fell inside. I hadn't realized just how exhausted I really was. I locked the door, threw the deadbolt, and then went up the steps to my bed. Scout and Jem meowed at me in greeting from the cat pile they had made in the middle of the bed. I sat next to them and scratched their little heads. Jem rolled over for a tummy rub. I started to feel a bit better.

After some thorough attention to my babies, I took a quick shower to get the stink of chlorine off my skin. I'd probably now associate that smell with death for the rest of my life. Once I was changed into my loungewear, I grabbed a bottle of cold water from the mini-fridge and slumped onto the sofa to drink it.

I was having a hard time winding down. I desperately needed to sleep, though. I would finish my water, diffuse some lavender oil, put on my ocean-sounds sleep app, and lie down in my bed.

I just hoped images of Thomas Banks with his gray skin and clouded eyes didn't haunt my dreams. In the morning, I planned to find out everything I could on the man and also check out the spa. I had a feeling that I was onto something there.

Standing, I stretched and walked to the balcony doors to look out into the night. The view from my room was spectacular, even in the dark. The moon illuminated the water that rippled just beyond the cliffs. It looked like a gorgeous night, and I wondered where Daniel Evans was headed for his run. The handsome mayor was probably the last person I should've been thinking about, but I couldn't help my hormones. He was pleasant to look at, and he smelled good, too. I was a sucker for a man who didn't smell like a cologne factory.

I took a long drink of water and then stopped, the bottle still on my lips. Beyond my patio, just past the walking path that wound around the hotel, was a figure standing barely out of reach of the light from the streetlamp.

It was a silhouette of a man, a tall man, facing my windows.

The hairs on my arms rose as dread surged through me. I was certain that whoever was standing there was looking directly at me.

I slid open the balcony doors and walked out onto my little patio. It took every bit of restraint not to call out, "Are you watching me?" But there was no need because the figure turned and ran into the darkness.

I jumped over the short railing separating my patio from the grounds and jogged to where I'd seen him standing. I turned and looked toward my suite. Yup, I could see inside my room plain as day, especially with my lights on.

To be fair, though, I couldn't see inside a few darkened windows in the same area.

I looked into the darkness where he'd dashed, hoping to catch sight of something that could identify him. I didn't see any figures out on the cliffs in the night.

Could the figure have been Daniel Evans? I hoped it wasn't.

I glanced down at the ground around the spotlight of yellow from the streetlamp—maybe there were footprints in the dirt. No footprints, but I did see a cigarette butt. A Marlboro. And it was still smoldering.

CHAPTER TEN

THE NEXT DAY, I was dragging at the concierge desk. I stifled yet another yawn. It was only ten o'clock in the morning, and I was fighting to stay awake.

I hadn't slept at all last night. After seeing the man watching me from the dark path, I had turned off all the lights in my suite and then grabbed a blanket. I sat on the sofa staring at the balcony doors, phone in hand and a knife nearby.

In my small kitchenette, the best weapon I could find was only a bread knife, but wielded properly, I knew I could do a lot of damage. Scout and Jem thought we were having a slumber party, so they joined me on the sofa. I knew I should've closed my eyes and slept, even for a few hours, but after finding the dead body and the threat I sensed from the unknown watcher, my sleep would've been nothing but nightmares anyway.

No stranger to all-nighters, when the clock hit four a.m., I did some gentle yoga, jumped in the shower, then popped several B-12 tablets and some ginseng. By six, I was ready to go to work.

My determined enthusiasm hadn't lasted long. Lois tracked me down, still annoyed at my interference in the sheriff's investigation. She'd instructed me to organize fifty gift baskets for the guests from the conference who had been inconvenienced last night. I guess she'd found out about my appeasement gift to Mrs. Lowry and thought it would be a great idea for all the guests. Though she didn't say so. I added a trip to the village to get gifts for the baskets to my list of things to do.

Before I left, I helped a couple book a romantic dinner cruise around the island. The couple thanked me and went about their day. Ginny shuffled up to the concierge desk a few minutes later.

She looked like she'd done an all-nighter at a rock concert. Her blond hair was shaggier, and the smoky green eye she usually applied with a deft hand was more smudged than normal. Combine that with the pattered tunic and flared pants, and she could've easily graced the cover of any boho magazine.

It had always bothered me that she could be scraggly and unkempt and simultaneously gorgeous. Whereas, right now, I looked like I hadn't slept in a week. Because of my pale skin, the bags under my eyes looked like steamer trunks. Blondes might have more fun, as the old hair-color commercial claimed. But our skin showed the world every little thing, too.

Ginny yawned. "So, I guess I'm your basket-making partner for the day."

I tried not to laugh. "Your mom's punishing you because you hired me."

She gave me a tired smile and nodded. "She's perfected the art of passive-aggressive behavior over the years. Dad used to say she had a PhD in paying penance."

"Yeah, speaking of your dad...I saw Lois in the hallway last night, and she was, uh, having a chat with him, I guess you could say."

Ginny rolled her eyes and gave a half smile. "Normal. For her. She just can't let go. I think it soothes her to feel like she is still connecting with him in some way."

"Actually, that makes perfect sense," I said and gave her a hug, even though it didn't make much sense to me that Lois was talking to a ghost.

Ginny didn't want to walk down to the village, probably because her three-inch platforms hurt her feet. She commandeered one of the hotel's golf carts, which weren't supposed to be taken off the grounds and definitely not driven into the village. Lois would not be happy when she found out.

Ginny drove too fast, and I was sure we were going to tip over when she took the turn at the bottom of the Park Hotel hill too quickly. We didn't, and she jerked us to a stop on Market Street in front of the Frontenac Island Bubbles Soap Co.

When we went inside the cute store, a bald man with a handlebar mustache came out from around the front counter and beamed at Ginny. He opened his arms to her. "Gin! I'm so happy to see you."

I rolled my eyes. I really disliked when someone shortened an already shortened nickname. It would be like if someone called me An, instead of Andi, which was already short for Andrea. It was a pet peeve of mine. When did we get tired of using syllables?

Ginny hugged him and then turned to me, gesturing first toward the man and then toward the shop. "Andi, this is Ben. He owns this place and handcrafts all the soap himself. Best soap on the planet, bar none."

She giggled at her own pun, which was also the shop's catchphrase and was plastered everywhere on the walls, the labels, and the products.

"Nice to meet you, Andi." Ben shook my offered hand. "Well, not all by myself. Corey does help once in a while."

The aforementioned Corey, I assumed, flounced out from the back room. He was definitely one of the most flamboyant men I'd ever seen, and I'd lived in California for many years. His jet-black hair ran down his back in a gorgeous braid, and he wore the prettiest silk scarf that looked hand-painted.

He offered a big grin and a wink in my direction. "I'm the genius behind this operation, and don't you forget it."

"Never." Ben grabbed Corey's hand, pulled him close, and gave him a big hug. "You wouldn't let me, even if I tried."

Corey laughed and then turned to me. "Girl, you have the most flawless skin. What are you using?"

"Thank you." His abrupt switch in topics had me flustered. "I use Neutrogena products."

"Mmhmm, I've heard they're the best for fair skin. Nicole Kidman swears by them." He nodded. "Do you know Nicole Kidman?"

"Ah, no."

"I thought you were some fancy LA lawyer or something. That's what Gin's always telling us."

I glanced at Ginny, who looked a bit sheepish. "I didn't say you worked with celebrities or anything. Just that you were a big-shot lawyer in California."

Corey waved his hand at me. "You know, you should set up shop here. There are lots of people you could help."

"Yes!" Ben chimed in. "The guy we use now is a complete waste of space. I swear he got his law degree in the bottom of a donut box, he eats so many."

"Besides that," Corey added, "he's definitely a bigot."

That piqued my interest, and I took a step toward him. "Is he? How? Did he do or say something to you?"

"There, that's what we need. Someone who takes an interest." Corey clapped his hands in delight. "You're ferocious, like a posh tiger."

The adrenaline rush quickly faded when I remembered that I couldn't practice here or anywhere for that matter. I wasn't licensed in Michigan, for one thing. And I couldn't get licensed anywhere while I was suspended and under investigation in California.

I sighed. "Yeah, I can't...I'm not practicing law right now."

Ginny must've picked up on my distress because she directed the conversation elsewhere. "So, can we get that soap order Lois phoned about? You know how she is if something can't get done."

"Oh, don't we know it." Ben laughed. "Let me go get it together."

When he had vanished through the beaded doorway to the back, Corey leaned on the front counter, a gleam in his eyes. "So, tell me everything about this murder. I mean, I can't even believe it."

"Yeah, it's a bit of a mess at the hotel right now. Andi was right in the middle of it. She knows more than I do." Ginny glanced at me. I gave her a tight-lipped smile.

"I need coffee. I'm just going to pop in next door," I said. I'm not a gossip. And lawyers are trained to keep secrets. Just because I'd vowed to solve this murder, it didn't mean I was going to blab everything I knew to every busybody on the island.

Without waiting for a response, I left the shop. Once outside, I took in a deep breath of fresh air. The overwhelming combined scents of all the soaps had given me a headache. On top of all that, I didn't really want to relive the story about how I found the body. It was still too fresh in my mind. When I closed my eyes, all I saw was the sallow, gray face of Thomas Banks.

I walked down to the corner and into the café. It was buzzing with activity inside. Lots of tourists but locals, too. The Weiss Strudel House café, I was told, was famous for pastries, strudel in particular. At the counter, I ordered a latte and an apple strudel. I took my order outside to get away from the constant gossip about the murder at the Park Hotel.

I sat on one of the decorative cast-iron chairs at a small, round, white metal table. It was very European and quaint. As I sipped on my coffee, I looked up, eyes closed, and let the sun heat my skin. Since finding the body, I hadn't been able to get warm. I was constantly shivering and rubbing my hands together as if I might start a fire with them.

"The way Lonnie tells it, the guy had it comin'."

I opened my eyes to see the two old men Ginny had pointed out playing chess at the dock the day I arrived. JC and Reggie were sitting at the next table drinking coffee and eating pastries. Reggie had flakes all over his chin from the strudel.

JC, cap skewed to the side, shook his head. "Still no reason to be happy the man is dead."

"Lonnie's not happy. He's just sayin', that's all."

"What's he just sayin', then?"

"That this guy was a two-bit crook. Into all kinds of criminal stuff. Lonnie owed him some money, and he nearly took a bat to Lonnie's knees when he didn't pay up right away."

"Did he finally pay the man back?" JC asked.

"You know it. And you can bet that my Lizzie had a hand in that. You know that girl takes no crap from Lonnie. I didn't raise her to be no doormat."

"Well, regardless, Lonnie's right. Sounds like Thomas Banks had it comin' to 'im."

I shoved the last of my pastry into my mouth as I got up and scurried back to the soap shop.

CHAPTER ELEVEN

WHEN I REENTERED THE soap store, Ginny, Corey, and Ben were still gabbing.

Ginny smiled. "Hey you."

"We need to get back to the hotel."

"We still got some time, I think. Nicole said she'd cover for you for a couple of hours."

"No, we need to go now."

She frowned. "What's going on?"

"Nothing. I need to get back to the desk."

"Really? I would've thought you needed a break from everything."

"I did. I've had it, and now it's time to get to work." I grabbed the big bag of soaps for the gift baskets. It weighed a ton, and my arm nearly pulled out of its socket. I nodded to Ben and Corey. "Nice to have met you."

Then I was out the door and jumping behind the wheel of the golf cart.

Ginny climbed in, frowning at me. "What's going on?"

"Nothing." I started the cart and did a U-turn, nearly toppling us, and then I was racing up the hill back to the hotel. "Lizzie is one of the housekeepers, isn't she? I met a Liz or Lizzie yesterday, I think."

Ginny frowned. "You have that look on your face."

"What look?"

"That one you always get when you're determined to get to the bottom of something. Usually something you should've let go of before it bit you in the ass." Ginny paused. "Lois won't like it if you keep poking your nose into this murder, Andi. She's already warned you more than once. You could be on your third strike already."

I shrugged. "Maybe I'm just pumped about making complimentary gift baskets for the guests."

"Andi, you're my best friend. I know you better than I know my brother, for Pete's sake. Confess."

We crested the hill, and I parked the cart in the designated spot near the golf clubhouse. I grabbed the big bag of soap. "Okay. I overheard Reggie and JC at the café talking about Thomas Banks." At her confused look, I added, "The dead guy."

"Oh, right."

"So, I guess some guy named Lonnie—"

"That's Lizzie's husband."

"I guess he had some shady dealings with Thomas Banks."

Her eyes widened. "You're not saying that Lonnie killed..."

"No. I just want to talk to Lizzie and see what she knows about this Thomas Banks. Could be helpful."

Ginny sounded just like her mother when she said, "Please, Andi. Stay out of this. I know you're curious by nature, and I'll admit that you're good at uncovering facts and putting them together. But you don't need to be involved in a murder investigation. Let the sheriff and his deputies handle it. I'm sure they've already questioned Lizzie. Leave it alone."

"But what if they haven't? Could be crucial evidence."

She shook her head at me as we walked into the hotel.

"What?"

"You need to get some sleep. This really has affected you."

"Look, I know I'm not a cop or anything, but...I don't know...I really need to help with this. I found him, Ginny. I feel like it's my responsibility somehow, to help solve the case." I didn't say that I wanted to do for Thomas Banks what no one had done for me: find justice. She'd have thought I was crazy. And maybe I was.

Ginny put a hand on my arm. "You are not responsible for what happened to Thomas Banks, nor are you responsible for solving his murder. You are a concierge. Your responsibility is to help guests have the best stay they can possibly have at the Park Hotel. If you want my mother to keep you on the job, you need to remember that."

Chapter Twelve

GINNY WAS RIGHT. I knew she was right, but that didn't stop me from wandering down to the basement when I had a ten-minute break from assembling the fifty gift baskets. The laundry was a huge open space with six industrial washing machines and a giant-size drying and folding machine. There were several folding tables as well and, of course, plenty of shelves covering one whole wall.

The Chamber Crew, as others around the hotel called them, consisted of four very close-knit women of varying ages who worked in housekeeping. When Ginny had introduced me a few days ago, I felt a bit intimidated. Especially by their leader, Nancy White.

She was the oldest of the four women and the most experienced and definitely the one who called the shots. She had an air of authority about her. I respected that, partly because she looked like she could bench press me and then toss me to the side without breaking a sweat.

Nancy was the first to greet me when I came through the door. No smile. Just a flex or two of her muscular, tattooed arms. "What can we do for you, Ms. Steele?"

"Call me Andi, please."

She crossed her arms, leaned against one of the folding tables, and waited for me to answer her question.

"I was wondering if Lizzie was around."

Another of the crew, one of the younger women, Tina Smallwood, came to stand beside Nancy. It was almost comical how diametrically different these two women were. Nancy was short and squat, with cropped blond hair that was more gray than blond, while Tina was tall and willowy, petite really, with long, straight, black hair that she came by honestly, I assumed, from her Ojibwe ancestry.

"What do you want with Lizzie?" Tina asked, also folding her arms and leaning on the table. They were obviously a united front.

"Just wanted to talk to her about something."

"This about the dead guy in the pool?" Nancy asked.

I considered lying, but I sensed she would see through it, and I gambled that she would appreciate honesty. "Yes."

"Shawn already talked to us," Tina said.

"Shawn?"

"Deputy Crowder." She gave me a *Hello, stupid* look.

"Oh, right, of course. Well, I just had a couple other questions."

Nancy narrowed her eyes at me. "Lizzie's not here. When she gets back, I'll tell her you're looking for her."

"Right." I knew she was lying, but I didn't blame her. I was an outsider and had yet to earn her trust or respect or anything really. "Thank you."

I turned to head to the exit. As I passed the other folding tables, my gaze skimmed over a stack of papers. I recognized the format of a legal document. Pretending to wipe something off my pants, I quickly skimmed over the particulars. It looked like Nancy's ex-husband was trying to force her to sell the house she lived in, claiming it was his before they were married. I could work with that.

"Are you having legal troubles?" I asked over my shoulder.

Nancy pushed off the table and came toward me. She scooped up her papers. "It's none of your business."

"I'm a lawyer, and I could help you."

She frowned. "I thought you were the new concierge until Casey came back."

"I am, but I was a lawyer back in California. I can't practice law here, but that doesn't mean I've forgotten everything I know. I've handled cases involving disputes over marital property before."

"Her stupid ex is making her sell her house," Tina offered. "He can't do that, can he? She's been in that house for thirty years."

"It depends. Did he buy it before you were married?"

"He did, but I helped pay for it. I put almost every cent I made into that mortgage."

"Then I can help you. We can prove your contribution and see what the judge has to say about it." I made serious eye contact with Nancy. I wanted her to know that I could fight for her.

She looked at me for a long moment and then nodded. "Lizzie's in the break room." She pointed to the door on the far side of the room. "Tell her I said it was okay to talk to you."

"Thank you." I smiled. "Tomorrow, bring all your bank statements, and I'll help you build a case against your ex. He won't have a legal leg to stand on after I'm done."

Nancy gave me a huge grin, revealing several stained teeth. But it was warm and inviting, regardless. "Hell, yeah," she said.

CHAPTER THIRTEEN

I OPENED THE DOOR to the break room and went in. Lizzie looked up from her cell phone and frowned.

"Nancy said I'd find you in here."

"Yeah, I'm on my break."

"I'm sorry to disturb you. I just had a couple of questions about your husband Lonnie."

She made a face. "What about him?"

"He knew Thomas Banks?"

Her brow furrowed deeper. "You're not a cop."

"I'm not, but I'm just trying to find out what happened to Mr. Banks. I thought maybe you could help me with that."

"Lonnie didn't kill him."

"I believe you." And I really did believe her, even though my legal background told me to suspect everything until she produced proof. She just had a way about her, a certainty in her statement. I continued. "But maybe the information you give me will help us find who did kill Thomas Banks. Maybe he had other shady activity at the hotel that had nothing to do with Lonnie."

"It wouldn't surprise me if he did. He was not a good guy."

"I've heard that." I pulled out a chair from the table and sat. "What kind of dealings did Lonnie have with Banks?"

"Lonnie borrowed money from him. We were in some trouble with our bank and the mortgage on the house. He got us some money so we wouldn't have to sell the house or anything."

I nodded. "That can happen."

"Well, Lonnie didn't know that Tommy Banks was going to charge us like forty-percent interest. I mean that's not right, is it?"

"No, it isn't."

"So, Lonnie couldn't get the money back to him right away. And that jerk showed up at the ferry and threatened to bash Lonnie's knees if he didn't pay up."

"What happened?" My fingers were itching for a notebook and pen. I needed to keep both in my purse in the future for situations like this when I didn't want to whip out my phone and record interviews or make notes.

"I got the money for him to pay Tommy back."

"When was this?"

"Six months ago," she said.

"And Lonnie didn't have any dealings with him since?"

She shook her head, but she didn't meet my gaze this time. "Nope."

"Have you seen Thomas Banks since then?"

She fiddled with her phone.

"Lizzie, you can tell me."

"I didn't see Banks. But Lonnie came to the hotel yesterday."

"Did he meet with Thomas?"

She shrugged. "I don't know, but he was really mad when he left."

"What time was this?"

"Around three, I think. I was on my break."

That could have fit the timeline. I really didn't want it to be Lonnie. I didn't know him, but I was starting to get to know Lizzie, and she seemed all right. Just a woman trying to live a decent life in whatever way she could.

I could check the security cameras in the lobby. They might have caught exactly when Lonnie arrived at the hotel and when he left.

"Lonnie didn't kill Banks. I know he didn't. There woulda been blood or something on him, right? I mean, from what I heard, the guy's head was bashed in. And Lonnie's clothes woulda been wet, right? Wasn't Banks found in the pool?" She reached across the table and grabbed my hand. "You believe me, don't you?"

"Yeah, I do." But believing her wasn't proof that her husband was innocent.

"Don't tell the sheriff. He doesn't like Lonnie much."

"Why's that?"

"Luke and I went to school together; we were sweet on each other for a bit. Then Lonnie rolled into town, and that was that for me. I fell for him hard. I think I mighta broke Luke's heart." She shrugged.

"I'm sure he doesn't hold grudges."

She laughed. "Yeah, you definitely don't know the sheriff."

After I left the laundry, I returned to the concierge desk. Nicole was covering for me, and she was just itching for a reason to complain about me to Lois and Eric. However much I tried to be nice to her, she was never friendly. I wasn't sure what she thought—that I was going to steal Eric from her? Which was laughable. But she wouldn't believe me if I told her that. She'd already made up her mind that I was a homewrecker.

When I arrived, her frown was etched so deep she looked like a ventriloquist's dummy. "You were gone longer than you said you'd be."

"I'm sorry about that."

"Uh-huh. Lois wants to help you, and you're Ginny's friend and all. But it's really not fair that I have to take time out of my day to cover for you. Don't expect me to do it again." Then she walked away.

For the next couple of hours, I fielded calls and helped a few guests with travel arrangements. When the desk wasn't busy, I scrolled through the hotel's Facebook page trying to find a picture of Lonnie Morehead.

I lucked upon one post about last year's Flower Festival. It had pictures of all the hotel staff and their families. I spotted Lizzie with her arm around a lanky man with a beard and mustache. He looked like the classic fisherman.

During all of this, I was thinking about how I was going to get into the security control room to find footage of Lonnie coming and going from the hotel. I wasn't confident that Joe, the head of security, was just going to let me have a look. I needed a way in. I could've asked Ginny, but she'd already given me the lecture about not getting involved in the investigation. I didn't really want to hear it again.

Which was when I spotted Eric crossing the lobby floor toward his office.

I stepped out from behind the concierge desk. "Hey, Eric. How are you today?"

"Fine?" He frowned.

"I need a favor."

"What kind of favor?"

"Don't look at me like I'm going to ask you for one of your kidneys."

He laughed. "The last time you asked me for a favor, Ginny got pissed at me for helping you plastic wrap her bed in the dorm that one night."

"Oh God." I burst out laughing. "I forgot about that."

It was the one and only time I had pulled a prank like that. My behavior had definitely been fueled by alcohol. Another something that I didn't normally do back then was drink. If I remembered correctly, my night of mischief had been prompted by a C+ I'd received on a term paper. Like all teenagers everywhere with big ambition, I was sure my life was over. So I threw caution to the wind and got drunk.

"She didn't talk to me for a week," Eric said.

"Really? I didn't know that. It was so funny, though."

He shook his head. "Ginny didn't think so."

"Well, I'm not going to ask you to plastic wrap anything. I just need access to the security office so I can help a guest who lost his wallet. He thinks it was stolen, but I'm betting he misplaced it." This wasn't *exactly* a lie. I *had* helped a guest with his wallet situation. And it was the best excuse I could come up with for looking at the security videos right now.

"Another lost wallet?" Eric said.

I nodded to avoid telling a flat out lie. He looked at me for a long moment, and I thought he might decline my request.

"Well, let's hope we don't find another body. One murder a week is about all Lois can handle," he joked. Then he said, "Yeah, okay."

I told Lane at the reception desk that I was going with Eric for just a moment, and then I followed him to the control room. No one was inside when he opened the door. I didn't need to be all clandestine about the situation. I could've just walked in. But I didn't know how the system worked, so having Eric with me, even under false pretenses, saved me from fiddling around and possibly breaking something. Then I'd have a lot of explaining to do.

Eric sat at the desk in front of the four monitors. He typed some command onto the keyboard.

"Are there cameras in the spa?"

He shook his head. "We just have cameras in the lobby, at the other entrances, and at the back for deliveries. We had someone try to break in one night back there. The cameras saved our butts."

Dammit. That was too bad. Cameras in the spa would have helped a lot.

"So, when and where?"

"The lobby, yesterday between two and seven."

He paused and gave me a look, and I wondered if he had recognized that as the time-of-death window for Thomas Banks. If he did, he didn't say anything and pressed some buttons on the keyboard, pulling up the footage I needed.

Peering over his shoulder, I watched on all four monitors the comings and goings of everyone through the lobby. I saw myself at the concierge desk on one of the monitors. I didn't look half bad on camera. My hair could've used some highlights, though. It was looking a bit mousy. "Can you speed it up a bit?"

He did as asked. My gaze flicked from monitor to monitor looking for Lonnie. At timestamp 2:35 p.m., I spotted him entering the hotel. "Stop."

Eric stopped the footage. "Did you see something?"

I looked over the image, making sure it was indeed Lonnie. Convinced it was, I asked Eric to keep forwarding. Then at 3:10 p.m., I saw Lonnie leaving the hotel.

"Stop!"

I peered at the monitor, scrutinizing Lonnie's body language. There was no way he had time to meet with Thomas, kill him, drag his body into the closet, go see his wife, and then leave. I sighed and straightened, no longer leaning over Eric. Although I wanted to find the killer, I was relieved Lonnie didn't have the opportunity, even if he did have a solid motive.

Eric frowned at me. "Are we good? Did you get what you needed?"

I nodded. "Yeah. I think so. Just keep going a bit more, though. Please." He continued to fast-forward through the footage. Then something caught my eye on the upper right monitor, the one that was nearest the pool and spa. "Stop."

Frontenac City Mayor Daniel Evans was coming out from that corridor at 6:15 p.m. wearing one of the spa robes and slippers. An hour before I'd found Thomas Banks dead.

Chapter Fourteen

A BIT RATTLED, I returned to the concierge desk to find
pandemonium erupting in the lobby. The women who worked in the
spa were freaking out and talking to the front reception about a pipe
bursting or something, as there was a flood in the men's changing
room. Lois wasn't on the premises, so Ginny and Eric came running.

"Did someone call housekeeping?" Eric asked.

One of the spa ladies, Carmen, nodded. "I also called
maintenance but couldn't get through."

"Damn it," Eric cursed. "I'm pretty sure Mick is off the
island for the day."

"There's no one else we can call?" I asked.

"I called Oleg from Gromeko Plumbing," Lane offered. "He
said he'd be here in less than an hour."

"In an hour, this lobby could be flooded," Eric said.

"You got tools?" I asked.

The three of us, plus Nancy and Tina from housekeeping,
went into the spa to see if we could at least plug the leak and

clean up the mess. Water pooled on the tiled floor of the men's changing room when we entered. My new shoes were definitely going to be ruined.

Nancy and Tina started mopping up the water as Ginny, Eric, and I searched for the source of the leak. There were ten shower stalls, a big private hot tub, a dry sauna, and a steam room in the area. The water had to be coming from one of those sources. Eric grabbed a wrench and headed toward the hot tub. Ginny marched toward the steam room, and I was stuck with going through the shower stalls.

I sloshed through the water and stepped into the first stall. There was no obvious bubbling-up of water near the drain, so I went to the next one. Then the next and the next. In the last stall near the inner wall, something on the floor caught my eye. One of the tiles seemed to be loose near the drain. Crouching, I tested it, and it wobbled a bit. Using the wrench I had brought, although I didn't know why I had—it wasn't like I knew how to use the darn thing—I pried it under the tile. The tile popped loose pretty easily.

Expecting to just see a concrete floor, I was surprised to find a bit of an open space underneath. Cringing at the thought of what might be in there, I reached in and felt around. Maybe something had clogged up the drain. I expected to find a massive clump of hair and soap flakes. What I didn't expect to find was a rolled-up towel jammed inside.

I tugged the towel out; it was larger than I'd first thought. There was something inside of it. I took it to the counter by the hand dryers and unrolled the white terry cloth to discover a man's suit jacket and pants—dark blue—and a white dress shirt. There was a dark stain on the right sleeve cuff.

Wishing I had brought gloves, I stuck my hand into the pant pockets. Both were empty. Then I checked the jacket pockets.

They were empty, but something poked my palm. I flipped the jacket around and heard the soft *tink* of something metallic falling onto the tile. I looked down, searching the floor. At first, I didn't see anything, and then something shiny caught my eye. I crouched and picked up a gold bar stud earring. It was heavy, and I imagined, as a pair, they'd cost close to five hundred bucks. Here was one, so where was the other? And what was it doing in the suit wrapped in the towel? A leftover from a wife or girlfriend maybe?

Ginny had come up behind me. "What's that?" Her eyes bugged out when she saw what I had discovered. "What the hell?"

"We need to call the sheriff."

CHAPTER FIFTEEN

SHERIFF JACKSON ARRIVED TWENTY minutes later with his two deputies in tow. Frowning, he peered at the suit and shirt I had splayed out on the counter.

"That's definitely odd," he finally said after I had explained where I found it and what had prompted the discovery.

"It's obviously evidence," I said. "The killer must've broken into the spa after he killed Thomas Banks, took off his clothing—as it was most likely soaked from pool water—showered, and then hid the evidence." I pointed to the stain on the shirt. "That's obviously blood."

"A lot of assumptions, Ms. Steele." He took off his hat and ran a hand through his dark hair. "What did he leave in? I think someone would've noticed a naked man walking through the hotel."

"One of the robes. Plenty of guests come from the pool and spa in robes and go back to their rooms."

He secured his hat back on his head and nodded toward Eric. "Are there security cameras outside this spa?"

Eric shook his head. "No, unfortunately. We only have cameras in the lobby and in the back near the delivery areas."

"There's an emergency exit door to the stairwell in the corridor. It goes to all the floors of the rooms," I said. "The killer could've walked up those stairs and gone back to his room without much fuss."

The sheriff looked at me, eyebrow raised.

"I checked the other night."

"Of course you did."

"At least I'm doing—"

Ginny slung her arm through mine. "Let's let the sheriff do his job, okay?"

I didn't say anything, allowing her to steer me away. I glanced over my shoulder and saw the sheriff putting the suit into a plastic bag. At least he was treating it like evidence. Jesus, what was it going to take? Me handing him a card that read, *Professor Plum, in the library with the candlestick*?

"You're welcome," I called over my shoulder.

He gave me a look but didn't respond. I imagined if we were alone, he'd respond all over me.

Before Ginny dragged me out of the spa, I heard the sheriff tell his deputies to search the place thoroughly for other items…and in particular, for a cell phone. That made my ears perk up. There must not have been a phone found on the body. They were looking for the victim's phone.

When we returned to the lobby, Lois showed up, none too pleased.

"What the hell is going on?" She glared at Ginny. "I can't even leave this place for more than a few hours, and it's falling apart?"

"Lois, if I may, this isn't Ginny's fault. The spa flooded because of something out of anyone's control," I said.

"I'm not even sure why you two are involved in this. You," she pointed at Ginny, "should be seeing to our business guests. And you," she pointed at me, "should be seeing to our regular guests, not off playing Nancy Drew."

"Mom," Ginny started but was cut off with a scathing scowl.

"Do your jobs, and I'll see to everything else," she snapped. And off she marched to the spa…to yell at the sheriff, I could only imagine.

I rubbed Ginny's back. "Don't worry about it. She's just angry at the whole thing. She's not mad at you."

"She's always mad at me. I can't seem to do anything right in her eyes."

"Well, at least she's here when you need her. I haven't talked to my mother in almost a year."

She gave me a small smile. "I better go check in on the meetings. I'll see you later."

I returned to the concierge desk just in time to help a panicked mother of the bride find a new dress, as the one she was wearing had a wine stain so large it would've taken a whole team of cleaners to erase. I called a boutique store that was thankfully still open and had them pick out several dresses in her size so she could go there, try them on, and buy one before the big event. The wedding was in a mere three hours outside in the garden. I loved night weddings, and I wished her well, after procuring her a ride to the store and back. She thanked me profusely, even coming around the desk and hugging me, then went on her way. The hug was nice. I didn't realize how much I needed one right about now. But she likely would've objected if I'd clung to her for too long.

While I counted down the minutes until I was done for the day, one hundred minutes and counting, I thought about the suit I'd found. It was a 44 regular and blue—cobalt blue, if I wanted to be completely accurate. So, whoever had worn it was definitely of average size. Not too tall and not too short. Not fat and not really thin, either. Basically, it did narrow down the suspects a little, but not by much. I was looking for a man between five-eight and five-eleven, 175 to 200 pounds, who would totally rock a cobalt-blue suit. I'd seen a lot of men wearing a similar getup coming into the hotel for the chamber of commerce meeting. But only one of them looked great in that blue suit.

Mayor Daniel Evans had changed suits, and I'd seen him leaving the area during the TOD window. He was looking like the most viable suspect, but what would he be doing with a low-level petty criminal? Just didn't seem like there was a connection. Or maybe I didn't want to see one since Daniel was handsome and pleasant. But so had been Ted Bundy, and look how that all turned out.

I also thought about the victim's missing cell phone. Would the killer have taken it? Possibly. Especially if there was something incriminating on it. Or had the victim dropped it somewhere in the pool area? The sheriff and his men had eventually searched the area, and obviously hadn't found it, or the sheriff wouldn't have mentioned it in the search at the spa. So where was it?

When six o'clock rolled around, I put up the closed sign on the desk and made a beeline toward the pool. The spa was closed, the doors locked shut, and it seemed the sheriff and his men were gone, so that left me all alone in the corridor. I waited for a few moments just to be sure, then used my key card to access the pool and went inside. Thankfully there was no crime scene tape for me to cut through.

I walked the pool deck, looking in every corner, under every chaise, and inside every potted plant. There was nothing to be found. I glanced into the open maintenance room, but my stomach churned. I wasn't sure I could go into the restricted area. It wasn't a large room, so I was certain it had been thoroughly searched. I decided not to go inside.

I turned to head back. I didn't see the evidence marker on the ground, which should've been picked up and taken away by the deputies, and I stumbled over it, losing my balance. I ended up on my hands and knees on the hard tile, my face just missing the chrome handrail that descended into the pool. What was it with me and shoes lately?

I grabbed the railing to pull myself up, and that's when I saw something glinting at the bottom of the pool. From this angle, I couldn't quite make it out clearly, but it appeared to be rectangular in shape.

I leaned forward and peered into the water. I moved my head back and forth, and saw that the glint came from the reflection of the light above. It was flashing from a reflective service. Like the screen of a cell phone.

Could it be?

If so, how had they missed it? These guys acted like the Keystone Cops sometimes. *Good grief.*

I quickly shucked my shoes, my pants, and my shirt. Biting down on my lip and peering into the water, I considered the situation and how crazy I was being right now. What if it was nothing but someone's watch, fallen off some guest while he swam….but what if it wasn't? I had to find out. Taking a deep breath, I dove into the pool.

I kicked hard to the bottom toward one of the drains. I could see something stuck inside the grate. The closer I got the harder my heart thumped. It *was* a cell phone; a piece of its broken plastic case was stuck in the drain. I grabbed it, worked it free, and swam up to the surface.

I broke the water's surface with phone in hand and a smile on my face. It quickly faded when three sets of eyes peered down at me.

"What the hell are you doing?" Lois demanded.

"Um, swimming?"

Mayor Lindsey gaped at me as I started to walk the steps out of the pool realizing too late that I wore both a white bra and a white pair of panties. White fabric that became see-through when wet. "In your underwear?" she sputtered.

My face went red, and I quickly sunk back into the water. But not before Mayor Daniel got his eyes full of a nearly naked hotel concierge.

And there was no mistaking the slight twitch of his lips as he pretended to cough into his hand.

CHAPTER SIXTEEN

I WOULD'VE LAUGHED AT the situation, as it was quite comical, but no one looked pleased. Well, except for maybe Daniel.

"I, ah, dropped my phone in the pool." I quickly showed them the phone, then smiled.

"So you just jumped into the water?" Lois asked incredulously.

"It's an expensive phone, and I couldn't get it with the net." I shrugged. "I didn't think anyone would be in here, so I didn't think it would be that big a deal."

The way she looked at me, I wasn't sure she believed the load of crap I was trying to feed her.

"Could I get a towel, please?" I pointed to the stack of towels behind Daniel.

He reached behind him, grabbed one, and handed it to me. I took it, wrapped it around me in the water, and then came out of the pool. Some would say it totally defeated the purpose, but I really didn't want to flash my wares to everyone again. That kind of stuff should only happen in private with an attentive audience.

"Well, you are definitely a determined woman, albeit unorthodox," Mayor Hamilton said, "I will give you that."

Her statement made me beam. It wasn't exactly a glowing compliment, but I was taking it as one. Although we'd gotten off to a rough start, I respected Lindsey Hamilton. She was a woman in power, which was not common. I'd done a lot of research on the topic for a client a while back, but then I'd done more for my own knowledge vault. At some point in my life, I thought I'd want to get into politics. Mayor Hamilton was leading the way for the rest of us.

"I'm sorry about this whole weekend," Lois said. "It's turning into one disaster after another. First the pool closure and now the spa." She flicked a deadly look at me, like it was all my fault someone had been murdered in her hotel.

Lindsey patted Lois's shoulder. "It's not your fault, Lois."

"You're doing an admirable job keeping everything together, considering the circumstances," Daniel said. "Despite the obvious hiccups, I'm enjoying my stay. My room is great, the food is top-notch, and the surroundings are quite…" his gaze met mine, "attractive."

Hmm, very brash, Mayor Evans.

"And the spa, Mayor Evans?" I asked. "How was the service there?" I knew it was bold, but I couldn't help myself. If he was playing a game, I wanted him to know that I knew how to play. Although considering the stakes, that might not have been my best or safest move. He knew where I lived.

He raised an eyebrow like I'd caught him off guard.

"When did you find the time to go to the spa?" Lois asked him with a chuckle. "We've been in meetings the past two days."

He cleared his throat. "I popped in for a quick...pedicure."

All three of us looked at him. He pulled at his blue tie, dropping his gaze to inspect some tiny lint on his pressed trousers.

"I like to take care of my feet," he explained. "There are a lot of health benefits to it."

"Well, you are a runner, so you need good feet," I said.

"That's true."

"And you run at night."

"I do." There was an amused twitch to his lips.

"And running along the cliffs can afford you some interesting views."

His eyes narrowed. "I suppose so, if one did run along the cliffs. Which I didn't."

I laughed because I couldn't keep it in. I'd been feeling uneasy about seeing him on video near the crime scene just before I'd found the body. And I'd thought he was the one watching me the other night. But he was innocent, it appeared. A pedicure. A jog that had not included the cliff area. In this case, I wanted to believe him, so I did. Sometimes it was good to be wrong.

"Andi? What has gotten into you?" Lois asked, none too pleased with me.

I shook my head, trying to rein in my mirth. "I apologize. It's been a long day, and I think I just need some sleep." I gestured to the pool and to my state of undress. "Obviously."

"Well, good for you, Daniel," Lindsey said, breaking the tension that seemed to be filling the room. "I wish Justin would do something about his feet. They're disgusting."

I fell into another fit of laughter. Lois and Lindsey joined in, and I considered the situation thoroughly defused. It was time for me to make my exit and investigate the mysterious cell phone.

I picked up my clothes and sloshed my way across the pool deck and out the door. Daniel's gaze was on me the entire time. I looked back to make sure my butt wasn't exposed. It wasn't. But he'd been staring at me for some reason, and I tried not to be uneasy about that.

Back in my room, I dunked the waterlogged phone into a cup of rice, hoping for the best. I had no way of knowing how long the phone had been submerged. It could be a total loss, even with high-tech equipment or a contact at the phone company to bring the data back to life, which I didn't have access to here in my room. But I hoped the phone wasn't damaged beyond the point of no return.

I quickly showered off the chlorine, changed into comfy lounge pants and a t-shirt, then sat on the sofa. Scout joined me, but Jem was sleeping on the floor in the last pool of sunlight, effectively ignoring me. He'd been grumpy lately. Probably because I'd been so busy and didn't afford him with enough scratches on his little belly for his liking. He could be a real diva when he wanted to be.

As Jem curled up in my lap, I pulled the phone out of the rice. It was a disposable—something a person could buy on the go—so maybe the rice trick was doomed. I turned the phone on. For a few moments, it seemed like a lost cause, but then I was rewarded with a lit-up screen and a couple of icons. Using the arrows on the keypad, I scrolled to text messages and pressed OK. The screen filled with what had to be Thomas's last three texts, all to the same phone number. I quickly jotted the number and the messages down on a piece of a paper in case the phone died later.

I'm here. You better bring me my money!
I'm not playin, meet me or else!
Meet me at the pool at 6 or everyone will know the truth.

I knew I should march down to the sheriff's station and hand over the phone immediately, without doing anything else. I knew I was courting trouble by searching through the phone myself. Sheriff Jackson could charge me with obstruction of justice or something, and he was the type of man who would do just that. Criminal charges wouldn't help me one bit with my license suspension board hearings, either.

Before I lost my nerve, I quickly punched in the phone number Banks had texted and waited. It rang twice then went to an automated voice mail. I disconnected.

I shouldn't have expected anything different. Maybe the owner of the phone was the killer. It wasn't like the killer was going to answer the call from a dead man's phone. The number probably went to another burner anyway. And he'd probably had already tossed it since it was tied to a murder victim.

Thomas Banks had been blackmailing someone, probably the killer—that much was clear. But about what? It was difficult to decipher just by the text messages. It could've been anything. An affair, embezzlement, a dark secret from the past. Any one of those would be good blackmail material.

Scout meowed at me when I moved, and I scratched her little black chin where she liked it the most. I picked her up and took her with me to the bedroom to change. "I know, I know. I should take the phone to the sheriff. You're right. As always."

CHAPTER SEVENTEEN

I WALKED DOWN TO the village since it was a nice evening. Along the way, I considered calling my parents. I really should let them know I'd moved across the country. But that would mean telling them why I'd moved. Which would lead to a discussion of Jeremy's embezzlement and how I could possibly have been so blindly stupid. I could feel the disapproval washing over me just thinking about talking to them. So I didn't. I'd put it off this long. The call could wait.

I passed the horse-drawn carriage parked to one side and recognized the mother of the bride stepping out with her gorgeous daughter in her very puffy wedding dress. The mother wore a simple but elegant teal gown that looked stunning on her. I was pleased to provide that small service to her.

That was one thing about the law that I loved: service to people. For people. I was all about the solutions I could provide, even if they seemed small and insignificant on the outside. I knew what it meant to the person who needed the help.

The sheriff's station was housed in an old brick building next door to the town hall. Both buildings looked like they'd been some of the first to be constructed on the island. Historic and just a little bit rundown, like many other buildings I'd seen.

I walked up the three steps to the front door and went in. It was bare but clean inside. One of the deputies, Shawn I think it was, got up from his desk and wandered up to the small front reception counter.

"What can I help you with?"

"I need to see Sheriff Jackson."

He narrowed his eyes at me. "You're from the Park Hotel."

"I am, and I need to talk to him. It's important."

"He's not here. You can come back tomorrow."

"Really? I can see him sitting right there inside his office." I gestured to the window behind the deputy that showed Sheriff Jackson behind his desk, eating what looked to be a hamburger and french fries.

Shawn didn't even have the courtesy to blush when he'd told me such a bold-faced lie. "What I meant is that he's busy and not seeing anyone right now."

I waved my arms in the air, making sure the sheriff could see me. He did. Despite the glass barrier between us, I could hear him groan in exasperation. Shaking his head, he set down the burger and waved at me to come in. I gave a sweet toothy smile to the deputy as he opened the half door so I could come through to the sheriff's office.

"What can I do for you, Ms. Steele?" Sheriff Jackson sighed as he leaned forward, putting his elbows on his desk.

I dropped the plastic bag containing the cell phone in front of him. "I found this in the pool when I was, ah, swimming. I'm pretty sure it belonged to Thomas Banks."

"You assume, or you know for sure because you went through it?"

I scrunched up my face. "The second thing?"

"So, your prints are going to be all over it."

"Yes." I sat in the visitor's chair which was just a hard wooden thing not made for comfort. Not surprising considering the man whose office it was in.

He ran a hand through his hair, which I was coming to identify as a sign of irritation. Especially with me. "Well, now we're going to need to take your fingerprints."

"That's fine," I said. I didn't remind him that I was a lawyer and my prints were already in the system in California. I didn't need him poking around in my business out there.

He leaned back in his chair and regarded me with narrowed eyes and furrowed brow. "You are quickly becoming the biggest pain in my ass I have ever personally dealt with."

"This pain in the ass just happened to find two crucial pieces of evidence for you, Sheriff, so, personally, I think some gratitude would be in order."

"If you want gratitude, go help your hotel guests find a good restaurant and leave the crime investigation to the professionals."

"There was blood on that shirt, wasn't there? The victim's, I'll bet."

"I really don't need someone who's watched too much *CSI* on TV thinking they know what they are doing."

"I never watch *CSI*. Too farfetched. Besides Grissom was way too charming to be in law enforcement." I sniffed.

He pointed to the door. "Tell the deputy to take your prints, and then get out of my station."

I stood. "Your position is an elected one, right?"

"Yeah?"

"Good. Now I know who not to vote for in the next election." I marched out of his office, slammed his door shut, and scowled at the deputy. "Take my prints, and make it quick."

Modern police stations have computerized equipment for fingerprinting. No messy ink and finger rolling and whatnot. But not here on Frontenac Island, where even the forensic techniques were historic.

While the deputy rolled the pads of my fingers along the ink pad, my gaze landed on a thick manila folder nearby. It was the case file. It had Thomas Banks's name printed in marker along the tab. The deputy proceeded to take each of my fingers and roll them onto the fingerprint card. As he did that, I thought about how I could get a peek into that file.

After he was finished, he handed me some paper towels to wipe off the ink from my hands. I smiled at him, then swung around suddenly and 'accidentally' knocked over the open ink pad. It landed on his pants. Black ink quickly stained his uniform.

"Damn it!"

"Oh my God, I'm so sorry. I'm such a klutz."

He grabbed paper towels and wiped at the ink, which just made it worse.

"You need to get rubbing alcohol on it. It will soak up the ink."

"Where do I get that?"

"There's probably some in your bathroom. I'd go and check. The longer it stays there, the harder it will be to get out. Wait too long and you won't be able to get it out at all. I don't think the sheriff will like that much."

Deputy Shawn rushed toward the back where I assumed the staff bathroom was. Now was my chance. I quickly opened the file and started thumbing through it, careful not to get my inky fingerprints on the papers, although the ink was practically dry already. The first form was the preliminary autopsy report. The final report would take a while, I guessed.

The preliminary report was a very clean-looking form, simply laid out with a diagram of the body, a description of the corpse, and spaces to explain external injuries, internal injuries, cause of death, and general notes. I appreciated that. Some forms were far more complicated than they needed to be. I breezed through the pages.

Thomas Banks, Caucasian, 29 years old, 5'10, 180 pounds, deep tissue wound on his left temple, skull fracture, water in his lungs. Cause of death, blunt force trauma probably caused by a blow to his temple with a heavy metal object with a pointed edge.

I wanted to continue to dig through the file, but I heard the deputy's footsteps coming from the back. I quickly flipped the file closed and took a distancing step away. I grabbed more paper towels and continued to scrub at my fingertips.

"I'll be leaving now," I said, then marched to the half door and opened it. I didn't look back, in case the deputy could read my guilty face.

Chapter Eighteen

AS I WALKED DOWN the stone steps from the sheriff's station, I was still wiping the ink off my fingers. I was certain the deputy put more ink on my fingers than was necessary. The sheriff probably told him to do that, just to be petty. My phone rang from inside my purse, and I scooped it out and answered it. It was Ginny.

"Where are you?"

"Doing an errand in the village." I stopped walking and pressed myself up against the wall of the café as a very drunk couple stumbled by, holding each other so they didn't fall. The girl tried to grab my arm, and I had to dance out of reach. "Whoa, there," I said, phone still at my ear.

"What?" Ginny asked.

"Nothing. Just making my way back to the hotel so I can eat and get some rest."

"And call your mother." Ginny said. She'd been bugging me to make the call, and I'd been ignoring her. Which was what I did now...until she got tired of waiting and said, "You can't put it off forever, you know."

I sighed loudly. "I know, Ginny."

"Okay. Well, Lois wants to know if you can help with cleanup after the keynote session tonight. It's going to be really busy, and catering could always use the extra hand or two."

I sighed again, wondering when I was ever going to be able to get some sleep. I'd thought moving to a quaint little island in the middle of nowhere was going to be the peace and quiet I needed. "Lois is punishing me."

"No, she isn't."

"No, she is, believe me. I'm pretty sure I embarrassed her earlier in front of the mayors, and now she's making me pay for it."

"What did you do?"

I couldn't believe Ginny hadn't already heard about my stint in the pool. "Doesn't matter. Tell Lois I'll be there."

"Okay. I'll see you later."

I ended the call and plopped my phone back into my purse just as I neared the chocolate shop on the corner. The smell wafting from inside drew my attention. My stomach rumbled like thunder. I hadn't had a chance to have any supper. My own fault really. Instead of eating, I'd been jumping into pools and collecting evidence I had no business collecting. I walked into the shop and bought a little box of salted caramels. Nothing like chocolate for supper.

As I was popping the third one into my mouth, I heard voices coming from the alleyway beside the chocolate shop. I wondered if it was the drunken couple having an argument. The girl sounded like she was crying.

"I told you not to contact me again." The man sounded extremely angry. "This has already gone too far."

"I know, it's just...I don't know what to do."

I kept walking and peered into the alley as I went. I spotted a man with thinning hair, average looking, and a pretty woman standing together. The man looked vaguely familiar, but they weren't the couple I'd seen earlier. She was wiping at her eyes with one hand, her other arm wrapped around her swollen belly. I didn't like the look of the situation. Despite the age difference, which was super obvious, they seemed mismatched. He looked like he'd spent a lot of time in a salon, and she looked like she hadn't washed her curly, dark hair in over a week.

"Everything okay over there?" I asked.

The man swirled around, his hands in fists. When he saw me, he seemed to forcibly relax. Did he recognize me? "Everything's fine."

The girl kept wiping at her eyes, not looking at me, just looking at her feet.

"Are you sure?" I took a step into the alleyway. I wanted to see the woman's face. I wanted to see if she truly was okay. I'd seen a few domestic problems over the years. The women usually got the worst of it if no one helped her.

He put his arm around her. "Just hormones. You know how it is."

I didn't. I'd never been pregnant. I was offended that he just assumed I would know because I was a woman.

Finally, the girl looked up and flashed a small smile. "I'm fine. Really."

I studied her for a long moment. I didn't think she was truly okay, but maybe they were just having an argument. Couples did that, and it wasn't always pleasant, but it wasn't something I needed to butt into. I'd had a few doozies with my last boyfriend, Nick. We'd yell at each other, but then we almost always ended up having make-up sex afterward. It got to the point that was the only way we'd have sex. Needless to say, we broke up. It wasn't a healthy relationship for either of us.

I nodded at them and continued on my way back to the hotel. The path up the hill was at a bit of an incline, but I needed the exercise. I hadn't been able to get into a regular exercise routine since arriving on the island. If I didn't get back to my daily yoga and hour walks, I was going to start packing on the pounds, especially since I enjoyed the food at the restaurants too much. It was dangerous how good the desserts were, especially the Bourbon Chocolate Cake. I really needed to stock my mini-fridge with fruits and vegetables to stop me from ordering the cake from room service at midnight, like I had the first few nights.

Once I got to the hotel, I went directly to the conference rooms. It was close to eight, and I didn't know when the keynote event was scheduled to finish. As I walked down the corridor, I spotted Daniel outside the main hall, pacing and reading over some cue cards. He pulled at his tie and cleared his throat.

"Hello, Mayor Evans," I said as I approached him.

He looked up at me, gave me a quick smile, but didn't say anything. Gone was the self-confident politician I'd seen earlier. He looked nervous, and he was actually sweating. His top lip beaded with perspiration. Not that I was scrutinizing his perfect mouth.

"Are you okay? You look a little…"

"I'm waiting to give a speech." He cleared his throat again.

"You seem really nervous."

He frowned. "Public speaking isn't really my forte."

"And you're a mayor?" I laughed.

"I know. Go figure."

"I thought all politicians were good speakers." I tapped my lips. "No, wait, that's not really true at all."

He laughed, and it seemed to relax him a little.

"The best advice I've heard about public speaking is this: don't talk right away, let the audience absorb you first, then make eye contact with everyone one at a time, and speak slowly to show you are in command."

He nodded. "That's good advice, Andi. Thanks."

Interesting. He remembered my name.

"I may not seem like the most level-headed person, considering what you've seen," I teased to help him relax, and he chuckled at that, "but I am actually pretty smart."

"I never doubted it," he said, then glanced down at his cards again.

He went over his speech silently, his lips moving as he read the words, I took that moment to look him over. Not that I hadn't already done that a time or two. I was checking out his suit. It had a similar cut to the one I'd found in the spa.

"Are you a 44 regular?"

"I beg your pardon?"

"Your suit. Is it 44 regular?"

"Yeah." He frowned.

"Did you bring more than one suit to the conference?"

"Why are you asking me this?"

"Just curious."

He scrutinized me. "I have a feeling that you don't do or say anything just out of curiosity."

"That's most likely true."

"The answer is yes, I brought two suits to the conference, in case one gets a stain or a tear or something. A little secret I learned the hard way when I didn't bring an extra suit once and a woman dumped a whole glass of red wine all over me."

"And that other one, the blue one, would be hanging in the closet in your room?"

His eyes narrowed. "Are you seriously interrogating me?"

"No. Just curious."

"Uh-huh. I think we already established that bit about your curiosity." He shook his head. "And the answer is yes, my blue suit is hanging in the closet. It was the one you accidentally spilled Kombucha on."

The door to the conference room opened, and Lindsey stepped out. "We're ready for you, Daniel."

He nodded at Lindsey and then turned to me. "Thanks for the interesting pep talk."

"Any time."

He adjusted his tie once more and then walked into the conference room. The door shut behind him.

I considered going back to my suite to eat a proper meal and then come back for cleanup, but I didn't want to waste a golden opportunity presented to me. I could go into the conference room and observe everyone inside. It was like having my very own captive lineup to identify the suspect. And without the sheriff's disapproving gaze.

So I didn't interrupt Daniel's speech, I entered through the door at the back of the room, careful not to let the door fall shut with a metallic clatter. I took up a position along the wall. From there, I could see every table. Granted, I could only see the backs of heads. Almost everyone had turned toward the podium to watch Daniel's presentation on cooperative building projects between the two towns.

There were ten tables arranged around the room, and about five people at each table. There were a few vacant chairs. I noticed that the majority of attendees were men, but I counted six women scattered among the sea of gray and navy menswear. A few of the men didn't wear jackets and just had on varying colors of shirts and ties. There was even one guy in a flouncy white blouse and vest. His mustache and slicked-back hair gave him a distinctive look, and I guessed that his name was Karl Neumann and he worked for the historical society. Ginny had told me about him. He was a notorious ladies' man about the island, and she gave me the heads-up.

Picking out likely suspects proved more difficult than I first thought. Especially since my attention kept going to Daniel as he walked around the front of the room and delivered his speech. He spoke slowly and smoothly, and I was pleased he'd taken my advice. Despite his claim that public speaking wasn't his thing, he was doing a fantastic job. Just about everyone in the room was engaged. All except one guy at the far table. He kept fidgeting in his seat and checking his phone.

I watched him for a few moments more, sizing him up. He was of average height and build. He wore a gray suit, and I wondered if he'd brought a blue one with him as well. At one point, he looked up, and our gazes met. There was something unreadable in his face, as if he was agitated for some reason. He looked away from me and glared at something else or someone else across the room. I couldn't tell who or what. Then he was back to checking his phone, with his leg bouncing up and down.

Interesting. I turned back to Daniel, who was wrapping up his remarks.

When he'd finished, the room erupted in applause. I noticed the fidgety guy was up and out of his seat immediately, heading out of the room. I tried to follow him, but everyone seemed to stand and move toward the doors all at once, like a stream of worker ants. By the time I was able to escape the room, he was long gone. I was all set to snoop him out when Lois stepped into my purview, a hand on her angular hip.

"I'm happy to see Ginny delivered my message."

"Yup, I'm here to help in any way I can."

"Good." She pointed to the big plastic bin that had been wheeled into the room. "There's the trash container. You can help put stuff in it."

Dejected, I joined the other waitstaff and started to clear off the tables. I set the dirty dishes and glasses on the provided carts. I gathered napkins and other trash and tossed it into the garbage bin. As I went around the room, I stopped at the far table where the nervous man had been sitting. I looked at his place setting and saw nothing out of the ordinary. I didn't know what I was expecting. A signed confession maybe would've been nice.

I pulled out the chair and searched on the floor for any garbage. My gaze landed on a small crumbled-up piece of yellow paper. It looked like a sticky note. I picked it up and unfolded it. Scrawled almost illegibly in blue ink was *Room 209*.

My heart jumped into my throat, and I had to sit down. Room 209 was the room Thomas Banks had checked into.

CHAPTER NINETEEN

I GRABBED ONE OF the waitstaff by the arm. The poor boy nearly jumped out of his skin. "Do you know who was sitting here?"

Eyes bugging out, he shook his head, then moved slowly away from me. I didn't blame him. I probably seemed like a mad woman right about now. I dashed out into the hallway, hoping to find someone who had a seating plan. Or maybe there wasn't one, and I'd never find out who the man was. Nope, I wasn't going to adopt a defeatist attitude. I had determination, and that counted for something.

I spotted Ginny in the lobby and pounced on her. She also looked a bit frightened by me. "Was there a seating plan for the keynote?"

"I don't think so. It was first come, first seated." She made a face. "What are you up to? You have that manic look again."

"I don't know what you mean." I surveyed the lobby and spotted several men in suits heading out the doors together toward the garden. "Is there an event in the garden?"

"Yes, drinks and music. I was able to book this local harpist. She's quite—"

"Okay, thank you." I made a beeline for the main doors.

"Andi?!" Ginny called after me, but I wasn't slowing down for anyone. I had to find this guy. I had to find out who he was so I could, theoretically, give the information to the sheriff to follow up on. Not that I would tell the sheriff until I was one hundred percent sure he was the killer, or at least guilty of something. I would not have Sheriff Jackson looking at me like I was a fool—again.

I joined the crowd milling about in the gardens near the large, round stone fountain. It was the classic fountain with a mermaid in the center spouting water from her mouth. There were several white garden chairs and tables set around the grounds. Fairy lights had been strung around the trees and trellises, and the bushes had been trimmed to resemble various animals, giving the whole place a very magical and enchanting ambiance. On a different night, I would've probably soaked it all up and enjoyed it.

Uniformed servers wandered the grounds with trays of champagne flutes and little desserts. I snagged a drink and couldn't resist a cherry tart—I needed to blend in, after all. As I sipped from my glass, I moved through the crowd trying to locate my target. I spotted Daniel talking to Lindsey and another man in front of me, so I reversed course. I didn't want Daniel distracting me. He'd done that enough already.

I did two complete circuits through the crowd, nodding and smiling at everyone, while disappointment slowly flooded through me. I'd missed my chance. Maybe he hadn't come this way at all. Upset, I snagged another glass of champagne, downed it, and decided to call it a night. I desperately needed sleep. The alcohol likely wasn't the best idea, considering I was operating on less than five hours of sleep and fueled by a few salted caramels and a cherry tart. My head was getting a bit foggy. I needed a bed, ten gallons of water, and my little fur babies to snuggle me to sleep.

I was making my way back to the hotel, on the cobblestone path through the lavish flower garden, when I spotted him—the fidgety guy. He was alone and heading toward the hedge maze. Although I knew it was a bad idea, that I had no business getting involved, that really I should just contact Sheriff Jackson and tell him what I found and my suspicions, I followed the man, stealthily like a ninja.

Before he disappeared between the three-tiered Victorian lampposts guarding the entrance, he glanced over his shoulder. I darted to the side to hide behind a giant hedge swan. I nearly poked myself in the eye with an errant branch sticking out from one of the swan's wings. After counting to three in my head, I peered around the greenery. He was gone, presumably inside the maze.

I approached the opening to the maze and took in a deep breath. It was creepy in the daylight, but at night, the maze was downright terrifying. My heart thundered in my chest. It felt like twenty horses were galloping across my rib cage. I peered to the left and then to the right of the maze, the yellow lamplight casting deep shadows across the greenery.

What the heck was I doing? This was crazy. I should just turn back and leave it up to the professionals.

But what if he got away? What if he left the island after this? I wouldn't be able to live with myself if I let a killer get away.

Patting my pockets, I realized I had left my phone in my purse back at the hotel. I was going inside the maze unarmed, so to speak. I thought about all my self-defense classes, visualizing scenario after scenario. I had on good shoes, ones that would make a serious dent in someone's shins. In the event that failed, I could run for miles in them. I was as prepared as I was going to get. I took in a deep breath and stepped into the maze.

Remembering my two failed attempts at the maze earlier, I went left instead of right. It wasn't a particularly difficult maze, but it did have a lot of dead ends and only two clear paths to the gazebo at the center. There was another entrance on the opposite side, and my fear was that he was going to just walk right through this and vanish without a trace on the other side.

When I reached the corner, I took a sharp right, went straight ahead, and then took another sharp right. That led me to a dead end, and I had to back up and retrace my steps. At the first sharp right, I took another sharp right. I felt like I was going in the proper direction now. Or I was going in a circle and would end up back where I started.

Throughout the maze, there was a scattering of Victorian-style lampposts, but the light did nothing to the thick darkness clinging to the hedges. Especially the ominous corners. I came to one and almost did a complete U-turn.

There was also a cloying dampness to the air, cool and sticky, like spider webs. I took another corner and stopped abruptly. The cold creeping of detached fingers peppered up my spine. I had the distinct feeling of being watched. Actually, it was more than that. It was deeper and darker than merely being observed. It was the sensation of being hunted.

I turned left, then zigzagged through a series of hedges. My pace quickened. Sweat dotted my forehead and clung to the little hairs on the back of my neck. I made another turn and ran into a dead end. I closed my eyes, trying to rein in my panic. I was okay. Nothing was going to hurt me out here. I could scream and someone would definitely hear me. Or maybe not, considering the harpist was still playing a haunting melody.

I backed out of the dead end and saw something flash ahead of me. I wasn't entirely sure what it was. Could've been a bird, for all I knew. Could've been my overactive imagination. Or it could've been a man intending to hurt me.

"Oh God," I whispered, gulping in air. A sweet scent of smoke filled my nostrils and mouth.

I had to get out of here. This was one of the worst decisions I'd ever made. No one knew I was here. If something happened to me, no one would know for hours, maybe not even until morning. Who would feed my cats?

Biting on my lip, I tried to remember the way I came. It was left, left, then right. Or was it left, right, then right? I took in a deep breath and pushed down the panic rising in my throat. It would strangle me if I let it. I counted to three slowly, then stepped forward, determined to get through this without having a heart attack.

From my other ventures through the maze, I remembered that there was a lamp at every proper turn. I looked for one, turned right, and then looked for the next. After finding three lamps and making three good turns, I was confident I was going to make it through. Hope swelled in my chest making it hard to breathe. Or maybe it wasn't so much hope as bravado.

I found one more lamp, made a left turn, and ran right into a dark dead end.

And I wasn't alone.

I yelped. As did two other voices.

Blinking the situation into focus, two faces formed in front of me. One belonged to the youngest member of the Chamber

Crew at nineteen, Megan. Who also just happened to be Sheriff Jackson's daughter—something I'd found out recently. The other face belonged to one of the waitstaff. He'd served me at the restaurant once. I was pretty sure his name was Patrick, and that he wasn't nineteen. More like twenty-nine.

"Oh my God," Megan panted, "you scared the crap out of us."

"Yeah, I know that feeling."

"What are you doing here?"

"Trying to get out of this blasted maze," I said, then looked at him and back at her. "And what are you doing?"

Licking her lips, she glanced at Patrick. "Please don't tell Ginny or Lois. They'll feel obligated to tell my dad."

No, that was the last crap storm I wanted to walk into. "Don't worry. I won't. But honestly, Megan, I would rethink your choices."

Patrick gave me a look. "That's kind of harsh, lady."

"I know, but seriously, you're like what…ten years older than her?"

"So?" he said.

"So, she's still a teenager with all the world's possibilities ahead of her. And you're still a waiter at a restaurant making minimum wage. You probably still live with your mama."

"And you're just a glorified butler. What the hell do you know?"

He was right. What the hell did I know? I was a failed lawyer running from my problems, hiding out on some island in the middle of nowhere, hoping everything would magically get better. I had two hundred dollars in my bank account, two suitcases of clothes, and a couple of cute cats. I didn't see my parents often. I didn't have any siblings or very many friends, and I'd never really experienced a full-on heart-shattering love. Not really the best example of success.

I sighed. "Can you tell me how to get out of here? I'm tired of running in circles."

"Go back, turn right, go straight, then go left and follow it along. You'll find the exit," Megan said.

"Thanks."

"You promise you won't tell my dad, right?"

"I promise. I don't think your dad would listen to me even if I did."

She nodded, which confirmed the sheriff's feelings about me, I guess.

Before I departed the area, however, I asked, "Hey, did you guys happen to see someone else go past here? A man. About yea high." I raised my hand to about four inches above my head.

"I think so," Megan said. "I don't know if it was a man, but it was someone about that height. I don't know why it's busy in here all of a sudden. No one usually comes in here at night. Now everyone's in here."

Thinking possibly I hadn't wasted my time, I turned and left the couple to go back to their making out, despite my reservations about doing so. I followed Megan's directions and could see the break in the hedge. I'd just about made it out, unscathed but empty-handed. I still didn't know who that man was or where he had gone, but maybe I could pick up his trail once I was out of here.

I was about to step out of the maze when something rustled behind me. I turned to see a dark form standing in the corner. At first I thought it was just my eyes playing tricks on me, from being tired and jumpy. Paranoia was the greatest trickster. But the black form moved, inching closer to where I stood.

Without hesitation, I dashed out from the maze. Unfortunately, I was on the other side, away from the hotel, away from the party and the people. Head down, I clenched my hands tight and made that split decision to run as fast as I could, not caring if I looked like a fool dashing across the manicured lawn with nothing chasing me. I would err on the side of caution. I took the first step forward when a hand clamped down on my shoulder.

I screamed.

Chapter Twenty

ON INSTINCT, I SWIVELED around, hand up to punch, knee to strike. I was rewarded with a yelp and a groan. But my triumph was short lived when I saw who was doubled over, his hand protecting his private parts a bit too late.

"Oh my God, Daniel, I'm so sorry." I went to touch him on the shoulder but thought better of it. He probably wasn't in a touching mood right now, considering what I'd just done to his groin.

The guy with him had his hand over his mouth, trying to stifle the laughter that was clearly bubbling up.

Daniel put his hand out toward me. I wasn't sure if it was to say, *I'm okay*, or to say, *Back off*.

He finally said, "It's my fault. I shouldn't have surprised you like that."

"I was on a bit of a fight-or-flight instinct high."

He straightened and nodded. "I should've known better. It's just that you looked like you were in distress or something."

"Yeah, I thought I'd seen something in there." I gestured toward the maze.

"An overactive imagination," the man standing with Daniel said with a bit of a laugh. "I'm the same way. Plus that maze is kind of spooky at the best of times."

I gave the man a wary look, and Daniel quickly introduced us. "Andi, this is Steve Bower. The owner of Bower Development here on the island. We're hoping to do some work together."

He offered his hand, and I took it. "It's nice to meet you, Andi."

"You, too." I frowned, trying to place him. He looked familiar—and not just from roaming about the hotel. Then it hit me. He was the man in the alleyway with the pregnant young woman. "Oh, right. How's your girlfriend?"

Now it was his turn to frown. "I'm sorry?"

"Earlier I saw you with that pregnant girl…in the village."

"No, I don't think so. I haven't left the hotel all day. You must have me mistaken for someone else."

Daniel chuckled. "Yeah, I was going to say…Pamela's pregnant?"

Steve laughed with him. "Would have been a huge surprise to me. Two ungrateful teenager kids in my house are enough for us."

I smiled to be polite, but I found Steve to be disingenuous. Almost smarmy. Maybe I'd been wrong about him, and he wasn't the man I'd seen in the alleyway. The couple was a distance away from me and in a badly lit back alley, and I had been tired. So it was possible I was wrong. And maybe Steve's kids were little jerks, and I was just being sensitive after having the crap scared out of me.

"What were you doing in the maze?" Daniel asked. "Seems like an odd thing to be doing so late at night. Alone."

"I was following someone. Maybe you saw him come out?"

Daniel frowned and glanced at Steve, who said, "I saw Nathan Hill maybe twenty minutes ago. He looked like he was in a hurry."

"Brown hair, average build, about five foot ten?"

He nodded. "Yeah, sounds like him."

"Do you know where he was going? Did he say?" I asked.

Daniel frowned. "Is everything okay? Did he do or say something to you?"

I shook my head, trying to appease his worries. "No, I just…he left something in the conference room, and I'm trying to get it back to him."

"Uh-huh. That's some kind of customer service you got going."

"Yup, all in the name of the concierge business."

He didn't look like he believed me. The stereotype was that lawyers were good liars, but really that's not the truth at all. Lawyers who keep their licenses to practice were not allowed to lie. They'd get in big trouble for lying. And I was a horrible liar. Which was obvious by the way Daniel regarded me now.

"Not sure where he was going," Steve offered, "But I know he likes to drink at the Victoria Pub in the village, playin' the big man. Maybe a bit too much." He chuckled. "Maybe he was heading there."

"Thanks." I nodded to them and speed-walked back up to the road leading down to the village. My feet were going to be some kind of sore when I finally was able to take off my shoes and actually get some rest.

Chapter Twenty-one

IT WAS JUST PAST ten o'clock, and the pub was in full swing, packed with people. A lively band was in the cramped corner playing something bluesy while some spirited couples danced nearby. As I pushed through the chattering and laughing crowd, I didn't know how I was going to find average Nathan in the sea of nothing but average men. Just about everyone had average brown hair, if they had hair at all.

When I reached the bar, I turned around and surveyed the crush of revelers around me. Everyone was talking loudly, trying to hear each other over the riff of guitar and drawl of lyrics coming from the makeshift stage. I heard bits and pieces of conversations that I found amusing.

The two young women in front of me were chatting about the prospects in the pub. According to them, there wasn't a man alive on the island who had any worth whatsoever. I hadn't been here long enough to decide if that was true or not. Daniel definitely had some value and appeal, except technically he lived on the mainland.

From others I heard brief snippets about the quality of the fishing season and the economic benefits of the upcoming Flower Festival, which was held every year at the hotel. I also heard discussions about the local groomer, Daisy, and musings about her sexuality, the fact that Monica Neumann, the local doctor, was just too good for anyone and that Pamela needed to do something about her philandering husband.

Then I heard the name Nathan, and my head jerked to the right to see, not surprisingly, JC and Reggie seated at the bar, drinks in hands, gossiping. That seemed to be all these two men ever did.

Which was fine by me.

"Yup, that Nathan Hill was never any good for anybody," Reggie was saying.

"Still, didn't see that coming. Who woulda thought he'd go that far?" JC popped a handful of peanuts into his mouth.

Reggie shook his head. "Let's hope Karl, the dumb fool, has a good hiding place. If Nathan finds him, he's going to get a bashing just like the last guy."

I didn't like the sound of that conversation. I needed to find Karl. Maybe he was in danger. I left the pub and headed down Main Street toward the town square. When Ginny had given me the lowdown about the island, she also gave me the 4-1-1 on island lothario Karl. He lived in an apartment above the historical society office, which happened to be on one corner of the main center of town about a block down from the pub.

The society was housed in an old whitewashed stone building built back in 1875. The little plaque situated on the wall beside the main door told me everything I ever wanted to know about the building.

The door was probably locked, as it was way past office hours, but I tried it anyway. Yup, locked. I went around to the back of the building to find wooden steps leading to the apartment upstairs. I climbed them and knocked on the blue painted door. The lights were on inside—I could plainly see that through the side window—but no one answered.

Cupping my hands around my face, I peered through the glass. I didn't see anyone inside, but the place was a mess. Kitchen chairs were knocked over, sofa cushions on the floor, papers and magazines everywhere. Either Karl was the worst housekeeper ever or someone had trashed his apartment.

I thought about calling the sheriff when I heard loud voices coming from the parking lot below. I quickly ran down the stairs to find Karl and Nathan dancing around each other, fists up in either defense or offense. I couldn't tell who was on which side until Nathan lunged forward and threw a punch at Karl's head. Karl managed to dodge the full impact of the blow, but Nathan's knuckles did graze his ear.

"Ow!" Karl grabbed the side of his head. "That hurt, you bastard!"

"It's less than you deserve!" Nathan swung again, but this time Karl was ready for it, and he danced out of the way. Nathan staggered forward and nearly fell onto his side.

So far, neither of them had noticed me, until I yelled, "I'm calling the sheriff!"

"Good!" Karl shouted back. "The bastard wrecked my place."

"You screwed my wife!" Then Nathan charged at Karl. He grabbed him around the waist and took them both down to the ground. By the time I punched in the sheriff's number, they were rolling around on the cement, hitting each other in the face, head, and shoulders. None of the blows looked like they'd landed. And the two of them pretty much looked like young boys having a slapping fight over who owned the best toys.

When the sheriff showed up ten minutes later with Deputy Shawn, Nathan and Karl were both on the ground on their backs, panting hard. Blood oozed from a cut above Karl's right eyebrow, and Nathan was sporting a fat lip.

"What's going on?"

"That guy," I pointed to Nathan, "was hitting that guy," I pointed to Karl. "Pretty sure that guy slept with that guy's wife. Or so he was screaming."

Sheriff Jackson shook his head and went over to talk to the two men. He stood over Nathan. "Is that true?"

"He slept with Rachel," he whined, and then he rolled over onto his side, pulled his knees up, and started to sob.

Sheriff Jackson looked over at me. "Little help here."

"What do you want me to do?"

"What do you do when someone's bawling like a baby?"

"I don't know. I don't have kids."

He shrugged. "Rub his back or something. That seemed to work with my daughter sometimes."

"Why don't you do it, then?" I said.

"Because I need to write up the report and interview the witnesses." To punctuate his remark, he took out a notebook from his back pocket.

I crouched beside Nathan. "You okay there, buddy?"

He wailed even harder. Snot ran down from his nose, and I had to look away. I reached over and gently patted his shoulder. I couldn't believe I had thought this guy was some cold-blooded killer. It was obvious to me now that he'd been agitated in the conference room because he'd probably just found out about Karl and his wife, and he'd been stalking through the gardens and maze looking for him. At least that was my assumption.

"So, when your wife slept with Karl…was that at the hotel?" I asked him quietly. I didn't want the sheriff to overhear me questioning the suspect.

Nathan opened his eyes and glared at me. "Yes, why are you asking me that?" He sniffled.

"What room was it in?"

He just glared and wiped his nose with the back of his hand.

"Was it in room 209?"

"207."

She pulled the piece of paper out of his pocket and showed it to him. "Did you write that?"

He gave me a funny look. "No."

"Do you know who did?"

"Stan Zhang."

"Who's that?"

"A private investigator." He sniffled some more.

"You don't happen to have his business card on you, do you?"

"How are you helping?"

"I'm probably not, sorry." I patted his shoulder a few more times and then stood. "Dump your wife. You'll be fine. Everything will get better."

Nathan stopped crying and got to his feet. The sheriff came over. "Karl's not going to press charges."

"See?" I said to Nathan. "It's getting better already."

"But you are going to pay for the damages to his apartment. Understand?" the sheriff said firmly.

Nathan nodded.

"Good. You can go. Get yourself cleaned up, have a few drinks. You'll feel better."

"That's what I told him."

Sheriff Jackson glared at me as Nathan stumbled out of the parking lot.

"What?" I shrugged at him.

"Why were you here?"

I considered lying to him but thought better of it. He wouldn't have believed me anyway. "I found a piece of paper with Thomas Banks's room number on it, and I thought Nathan wrote it, and he was acting all agitated and nervous at the conference meeting, so I tracked him down, and ended up here, and saw these two fighting, and then realized that 7s can look like 9s."

He shook his head. "Why are you always in the middle of everything?"

"Dumb luck." I put up my hand the moment he opened his mouth. "And if you say something obnoxious right now, I'm way too tired to be polite in return."

"I was going to suggest that you go back to your room at the hotel, have a hot bath, some tea, and go to sleep. You've had a really long couple of days."

I blinked blankly at him for a moment, surprised. "You know, I *have* had a long few days. Thank you. I will go back to the hotel."

"Do you want an escort back? It's late."

"Do you have one of those fancy golf carts, too?"

He smiled, and it nearly knocked me over. "Nope. I got a real vehicle. Only two on the whole island, and the other one's an ambulance. Only the finest for Frontenac Island Sheriff's Department."

I returned his smile, pleasantly surprised to have witnessed it. I wouldn't have believed his lips could turn up instead of down. "I will take you up on that. My feet hurt."

Fifteen minutes later, I was safely in my suite at the hotel. Deputy Shawn had given me a ride up the hill. And I was almost, *almost* disappointed that Sheriff Jackson hadn't escorted me himself. The moment I opened the door, my cats were winding around my legs, begging for food. I opened a couple of tins of shredded chicken, their favorite treat, and set it on the counter for them. Once they were eating, they totally forgot about me.

I dragged my butt into the bedroom to change into my pajamas, my assumption about my feet fully realized. They ached something fierce, and I went into the bathroom and ran some hot water into the tub. I sprinkled some bath salts into the water, then sitting on the edge, submerged my feet. The second my skin hit the hot water, I moaned with relief.

As I soaked my feet, I closed my eyes. I would be out like a light the moment my head hit the fluffy pillow on my bed. That was one big bonus of living in a hotel—the mattress and pillows were a dream. Plus, someone else did the laundry.

My phone trilled from the vanity's counter. I picked it up to see who was calling, hoping beyond hope that it wasn't Lois bawling me out for leaving cleanup early. Or worse, my mother. It was an unknown name and number, but it could've been anyone. I didn't have everyone from the hotel in my contacts yet. It could've been the sheriff, for all I knew. I answered, just in case.

"Hello?"

"Hello, Andi."

It was my old boss, Jeremy, the gambling thief who destroyed my career along with his. I was so astonished that I fell backward off the edge of the tub and smacked my head on the toilet.

Chapter Twenty-two

"HELLO? ANDI?"

Sitting up against the toilet, I rubbed at my head where I'd no doubt find a big lump in the morning. Reluctantly, I put my phone back to my ear.

"Andi? You there?"

"Why are you calling me, Jeremy?"

"Because I need to apologize to you. I'm so sorry this happened."

"Nothing *happened*, Jeremy. You did this. You, and no one else." *About damned time you apologized, too.* I sniffed. "You're sorry you got caught, you mean."

"This sucks for everyone involved."

"Yes, you've ruined my life as well as yours."

"They shouldn't have suspended you like that."

Why did I get the feeling that he wasn't actually apologizing but trying to get me to feel some kind of sympathy for him? Like somehow we were in this together. *Puh-leease.* I got to my feet and walked out of the bathroom.

"What do you want?"

"I went by your place. I brought over a bottle of wine and a gift basket from Patty Cakes. The little cream cheese cupcakes were your favorite, right?"

"Then I guess you figured out I don't live there anymore."

He chuckled. "Yeah, I guessed that when a very large black man with a ring through his nose answered the door."

My stomach grumbled. It was probably remembering those amazing cupcakes from my favorite bakery down the street from my old apartment. I went into my kitchenette, opened up the mini-fridge, and took out the small basket of blueberries. They'd have to do.

"I'm hanging up, Jeremy. Don't call me again."

"Wait! Where are you, Andi? I need to see you. There's something I—"

"Don't be ridiculous. Goodbye, Jeremy. I'm blocking your number." I ended the call amid more of his protests, but I didn't care what they were. Nothing he could say to me would make what he did okay. Or make me forgive him. Not only did he steal from his clients, people who trusted him, but he ruined everyone who had ever worked with him. We were all guilty by association. Unfairly condemned for what he did. Especially me. I'd been ostracized from the legal community, and I could still get disbarred.

And why the heck would he be contacting me? I'm sure his lawyer would've told him not to talk to anyone associated with the case and the firm. What was he up to? It had to be something hinky. I knew without a whisper of doubt that he didn't call to see how I was doing. He didn't care about me one whit. He'd already proved that much.

After I'd found out about his embezzlement, I scrutinized every interaction we'd ever had, every conversation, everything, to find out why, to find out what I could've done to prevent this disaster. And the realization I came to was…nothing. I couldn't have done anything to fix this. He'd been masterful at hiding his theft.

But I'd seen other signs—how he'd manipulated me and used me. Everything he'd ever said to me, or given to me, was about him, how it praised him, how it benefited him. Classic signs of a narcissist.

I'd been blind to his narcissistic personality at the time because I'd enjoyed the accolades he favored me with. I was new to the practice and so desperately wanted to succeed. The subtle compliments he gave me, the illusion that he was helping me, grooming me to one day become a partner at the firm. Something he knew I wanted and had been devoting all my time and energy to achieve.

His helpful behavior had been false. All of it. And I didn't see it at the time. Which made me feel stupid and duped. I'd never forgive him for any of it. I don't know why he'd care whether I forgave him or not, either.

I took my blueberries and sat on the sofa. All notions of sleep had left my mind. My body was still exhausted, screaming at me to lie down to rest, but my head had too many thoughts racing through it begging for attention. I needed to write them down so I didn't have to hold them in my tired brain.

I grabbed a pen and the pad of lined paper on the coffee table and started to make a list. List-making always calmed me and gave me focus. There was a connection between the brain and handwriting that had been proved by scientists. But I had always known the connection worked for me.

First, what I knew or had good reason to believe about the murder so far:

1. Thomas Banks, low-level criminal, died Friday between two and seven p.m.
2. Died from blunt force trauma to the head. Where is murder weapon?
3. Definitely had been in the water, so assailant had to have dragged him out and stored him in utility room.
4. The assailant broke into (??) spa, hid his wet clothes in shower.
5. The assailant left in a bathrobe (??) and used stairwell to go to one of the floors and one of the rooms (??)
6. Assailant is of medium build and average height.
7. Thomas was blackmailing someone, probably someone at hotel.

Wow, I really didn't know much of anything.

I set the pen down and ate more berries. Scout jumped up on the table and decided that she wanted the pen and knocked it onto the floor. I tried to pick it up, but she was too quick. She had it in her mouth and dashed around the room before I could grab her. I wouldn't have been surprised if she had a little stash of pens somewhere in the suite. She used to collect them back at the apartment. She liked to hoard paperclips as well. I was always running out and buying new ones.

Maybe she was just telling me to give it up. I was just about there myself. I had no business investigating a murder. It was just another way for me to avoid my problems. To ignore the fact that I might not ever be able to practice law again.

I got up and went to the mini-fridge to search for any leftover chocolate cake. There wasn't any, and I glanced at my phone and wondered if it was too late to order room service. *No, Andi.* I shook my head; I couldn't cave. I had to stop eating my stress and feelings away. Instead of grabbing my phone, I grabbed my laptop from my bedroom and returned to the sofa. I would do some research instead. I'd always been good at that. Jeremy used to say I could find out anything about anyone. Too bad I hadn't used those skills to expose him.

Instead of typing *Thomas Banks* into the search bar, I typed *Daniel Evans*. The first thing I found was the home page for Frontenac City. I clicked on his picture and read over his bio. He wasn't married and had no children. He'd been mayor for the past two years and before that was a local business owner. I was curious about what kind of business he'd owned, so I fell down the rabbit hole of social media and discovered where he'd gone to school, when he graduated, and that he once owned a construction company.

Now all I had in my mind were images of a shirtless Daniel pounding nails into a wooden frame of a home for Habitat for Humanity. I didn't know if he ever worked for Habitat for Humanity, but I wanted to picture him that way. The attractive man with the heart of gold.

"Andi, this is *not* helping," I said aloud. I sighed and went back to the browser's search bar and typed in *Thomas Banks*.

There had to be something in the dead guy's past that would help me figure out who he was blackmailing and why. It was amazing what a person could find just using Google properly. After supplying some inventive search terms, I got an address for him in Michigan. I investigated that and found a woman attached to that address who had the same last name. Helen Banks. Must've been some relation.

I searched *Helen Banks* and got back an obituary. The obit revealed that Helen had died a few years ago after a long battle with cancer. She was survived by her son Thomas and her daughter Sasha. So Thomas had a sister. I searched for *Sasha Banks*.

Majority of the entries were about a wrestling star named Sasha Banks. She was definitely not the girl I was looking for. I clicked on images, and of course, most of the pictures were of the vivacious, purple-haired wrestling diva.

I kept scrolling through the thousands of pictures until I found one nestled deep among the others—a simple photo of a dark-haired woman. I clicked on it, and it took me to a social media account for some writer from Canada. She wrote romance novels, and the picture was from a conference she'd gone to in Las Vegas. I went through the rest of her pictures, but after a few too many cat and food photos, I concluded this was not the Sasha I was looking for.

I shouldn't assume Sasha still had the same last name as Thomas. She could've been married and moved away anywhere. But surely there had to be more than one obit to connect the siblings. So, I searched *Thomas Banks Sasha Michigan* to see what else I could find. Old school photos would be a perfect thread to unravel. But nothing useful came up.

I leaned back in the sofa and considered what else to check when Jem started hissing and spitting at the balcony window. Jem had Savannah blood in him somewhere, and when he arched his spotted back like a ferocious bobcat, he could be downright frightening.

I got up to see what he was mad about. When I neared the glass, he puffed up to double his size and made a low yowling sound in the back of his throat. Scout had now joined in on the fervor. The racket was not helping my headache at all.

I pressed my face to the window but couldn't see anything out on my deck. I thought maybe there was another cat or a dog or some other animal. I wasn't sure what kind of wild animals there were on Frontenac Island. I'd seen squirrels and rabbits running around on the hotel grounds, as there were a lot of trees and plants to feed on. I hadn't seen any bigger game, like foxes or raccoons. I put in a mental note to ask Ginny next time I saw her, just for my own information.

As I kept peering through the glass, I thought I saw some movement by the bushes next to my deck. Another animal of some sort outside was the most likely instigator of Jem's reaction. I waited and watched to see if I could spot the telltale glow of glassy animal eyes. The bushes stopped moving, so I backed up.

I looked down at my cats. They were still puffed up but had stopped yowling. "Whatever it was, I think it's gone. You guys can relax now."

Like a bolt of lightning, Jem jumped at the window. I looked up just as a large stone hit the glass. The impact of it made me jump backward. My heart leapt into my throat, and my whole body shook. The balcony door now displayed a spider web of glass right where my face had been.

CHAPTER TWENTY-THREE

"IT WAS A WARNING Ginny. Someone doesn't want me looking into the murder."

"*No one* wants you looking into the murder, Andi," Ginny said wryly. "But you don't know that's what happened. It could've been just kids playing around."

I gave her a look. "Kids? Do you really think kids are going to toss a rock at my window while I'm standing there in the middle of the night?" I took another sip of the whiskey Ginny had brought with her, claiming it would calm my nerves. "No, this was definitely a warning. He was watching me before he threw the rock."

Ginny's eyes grew big as saucers. "You're scaring me, Andi."

"We should be scared. There is a murderer in this hotel."

She hugged her knees to her chest while we sat on the sofa. "I guess I never thought of it that way. Murders aren't supposed to happen on this island. Frontenac is a vacation spot. It's where people come to have fun, not to kill each other."

"Murder happens everywhere. There are bad people doing bad things everywhere." I rubbed Scout's little head for comfort. "I think he was watching me the other night as well."

Ginny sat up straight. "What? Why didn't you tell the sheriff? This is serious."

"Do you know anyone on staff who smokes?"

She shrugged. "A few people, I guess. A few of the Chamber Crew, Mick the maintenance guy, Lane at the front desk. Those are all I can think of offhand. But there's probably more. They can't smoke inside the building, but they do smoke outside on the grounds."

"Does Mayor Evans smoke?"

She gave me another look. "How should I know? Wait…why? Do you think it was him?"

"I don't know."

Ginny took a sip of whiskey and shivered. "We should call the sheriff."

"No, I think Sheriff Jackson has had enough of me nosing around in his business. He's made that clear."

"What are you going to do?"

"Well, I'm definitely not going to stop digging. I must be on the right track somewhere. The killer knows who I am and where I live, so I must've talked to him at some point."

"You're not making me feel better about this whole thing when you say stuff like that."

I got to my feet and paced the room. "I must be close to the truth. He wants to warn me off. Now I just have to put it all together. But I'm missing something."

"Well, we have to tell Lois something. She's going to freak when she sees the window. And we have to get it replaced as soon as possible, which isn't all that easy to do here during the height of the tourist season."

"She already thinks I'm a screwup, so it won't be a stretch if we tell her I accidentally broke the window. Especially if I offer to pay for it." I didn't have the money to replace the window, but I didn't know what else to do. I certainly couldn't afford to get fired again.

"You can't be the screwup," Ginny said with a wry shrug. "There's only room for one in this family. And I'm it."

I stopped and looked at Ginny, appreciating that she considered me family. I realized that I had not properly thanked her for doing everything she'd done for me. At my most vulnerable, she had opened her arms and hugged me tight without even touching me.

I plopped down on the sofa beside her and took her hand. "I love you, you know that, right?"

She smiled. "I know. How could you not?"

I laughed and squeezed her hand. "So now what?"

"Now we have a slumber party. Just like college."

"I hope you don't still snore."

"What are you talking about? I don't snore."

For the next half hour, we sat on the sofa, sipped the whiskey, and reminisced about our days and nights in college. I knew she'd stayed for my benefit. To keep my mind off the fact that someone had tried to hurt me. If that rock had broken the glass, it would've hit me right in the face. That was no accidental toss of some innocuous object. It was meant to hurt me or scare me, at the very least. And I had to admit it did.

But throwing a rock against my window wasn't going to stop me. I was too darn stubborn for that to work.

Chapter Twenty-four

WHEN THE ALARM ON my phone buzzed at six, I rolled over onto my side and nearly smacked Ginny in the face with my arm. She was still snoozing beside me on the bed and didn't stir. I'd forgotten she could sleep through Armageddon.

I grabbed my phone, turned off the alarm, then sat up. My head ached something awful. It was likely the combination of smacking it on the toilet and drinking too much whiskey. I wasn't a drinker, so having even the small amount I did was enough to give me a horrible hangover. Which wasn't fair, since I never got to experience the lovely floaty high of being drunk the night before.

I went into the bathroom to take a painkiller for my throbbing head, then went back to the bed and poked Ginny. She groaned and rolled over, pulling the covers up over her head.

"C'mon. If I have to get up, so do you." Technically, today should've been my regular day off, but because of the ongoing chamber of commerce convention, Ginny had volunteered me to join in on the golf tournament. She'd told Lois that I was a great golfer and had lots of experience.

I definitely wasn't a great golfer, but I had played with the partners and with clients. Jeremy used to love doing business on one fancy golf course or another. He'd made sure I had plenty of lessons. I got good enough not to embarrass him or the firm, but not so good that I could beat any of them, either.

I grabbed the blanket and pulled it off Ginny. "Up and at 'em, sunshine."

She opened her eyes and blinked sleepily at me. "You are a meanie."

"Yup, I'm horrible." I smiled at her. "Thanks for staying with me last night."

"Any time." She rolled into a sit. "I'll make sure someone comes in and replaces the balcony door while you're out putting those greens like a golf pro."

I threw one of the pillows at her and then retreated into the bathroom to shower. Last thing I wanted to do was to go play nine holes of golf with a bunch of people I didn't know. But I had to go if I wanted to stay employed at the hotel. What I really wanted to do was to continue my search for Sasha Banks. Maybe I would discover something that would prove useful to find the killer or at least a solid motive.

On my way out the door, I remembered that I hadn't called my mother. Briefly, I considered calling while I walked. But if she picked up the phone, it would lead to a longer conversation than I had time for. Okay. So I was making excuses. And the longer I put it off, the more difficult it became to make the call. Still, I didn't have the time at that moment.

By eight o'clock, I was standing with Justin Hamilton, Mayor Lindsey's husband, and Pamela Bower, Steve Bower's

wife, by our cart waiting on our fourth. We were to be the
second team to tee off, and we needed to be on the first hole
ASAP.

"Oh, here he is," Justin said, and I turned to see Daniel
walking toward us, looking stupidly good in a pink-gray-and-
white-striped polo and gray pants. How could a man look that
good in golfing apparel? Didn't seem possible.

"Sorry I'm late," he said.

Justin shook his hand, and then Daniel turned to shake
Pamela's. "Good to see you, Pamela. It's been a couple of
years."

She smiled, but it didn't quite reach her green eyes. "It's
always a pleasure, Daniel. Steve tells me we almost have a deal
to do some building on the mainland."

"Yes, just a few more details to iron out, but it seems
promising."

He looked at me, and I had to fight the urge to smooth down
the blue-and-white-patterned golf skirt that I'd borrowed from
Ginny. She was an inch or two shorter than me, so what was a
knee-length skirt to her was one that I wouldn't dare bend over in.

"Good morning, Andi. Nice to see you without your fists and
knees up."

Justin and Pamela gave us a look.

Daniel explained, "We had a bit of a misunderstanding last
night."

"How's your, um…leg this morning?" I couldn't resist. The
man was just too easy to tease.

"Fine. Thank you for asking." He gave me one of his
disarming smiles, and it worked. "Shall we?" He jumped into the
cart, and we followed suit. Justin got behind the wheel. Pamela
and I slid into the back.

Pamela seemed like a bit of a cold fish, but I hoped she would warm over the course of the day. If not, this was going to be a long nine holes. I looked her over, taking in her shiny blond locks, pulled back into a severe high ponytail, and her perfect heart-shaped face. She was probably close to forty, but I imagined she'd paid a lot to look barely thirty. In fact, she looked and smelled like money. I knew the type. I had helped several clients like her diversify their massive fortunes.

"I met your husband last night," I said, hoping to break the ice.

She gave me a simple eyebrow raise as a response.

"I ran into him with Daniel. They were walking by the hedge maze." Still nothing. "Have you been through the maze?"

"No. I'm not much for gardens." Her gaze moved past me to the golf course as we neared the first hole. It was a beautiful course, lush and green, with the expanse of the lake framing it perfectly. It was probably one of the prettier courses I'd played.

Thawing Pamela out wouldn't be easy. I needed a pickaxe to chip away at her stone-faced behavior. "Are you enjoying the conference?"

"These things aren't really for enjoyment. They're for making deals."

I nodded. "You run the business with Steve?"

She looked at me then, and her upper lip came up a bit. It wasn't quite a sneer. More smirk-like. "I *am* the business."

Justin stopped the cart, and she was the first one out, grabbing her clubs. She hobbled to the tee box—looked like she had a bit of a limp. I hadn't noticed that earlier. She took out a tee and set up her ball. I guess she was going first. She adjusted her stance, pulled back her club, and swung. There was the crack of the club hitting the ball, and then it was soaring through the air. A great shot.

Justin teed up next. While he did, Daniel leaned against the cart next to me. "Do you play golf a lot?"

I shrugged. "I've played my fair share."

"Really?"

"Don't look so surprised. I used to be a hotshot lawyer in California, remember? How do you think we got business done?" I grabbed a club and set up my shot. I lined up, squared my shoulders, and swung my driver. I was rewarded with the beautiful sound of a perfect shot. I watched as it soared, arced, and landed right next to the green, closer than anyone else had hit so far. Daniel chuckled as he went by me to set up.

The next two holes went on without a hitch. We were all playing fairly well. As a team, I imagined we were crushing it. Both Daniel and I were running one under par. On the fourth hole, Pamela sliced and sent her ball into the thicket of trees. I volunteered to help her find her ball. Lois would be proud of me, going above and beyond for a guest. I'd tell her when we were done so I could claim some suck-up points with her. I feared my job wasn't on very steady legs right now.

As we chopped at the underbrush looking for the telltale flash of white, I decided to try to pump Pamela for information about her husband. I knew that he'd lied to me the other night. I was certain I saw him in the village with the pregnant girl. And I wanted to know why. Well, if it was anything other than my first guess—that he was probably having an affair with the girl and got her pregnant.

Which in my mind was one hell of a legitimate reason to be blackmailed. Might even drive a man to murder, I figured.

"Have you and your husband been staying at the hotel during the conference?"

"No. That's Steve's thing. I have a perfectly good house outside the village, so why would I pay to stay at the hotel?" She sighed. "I have other responsibilities besides drinking irresponsibly with a bunch of silly men. Raising teenagers is a thankless job."

I nodded. "Your husband basically said the same thing last night."

Her eyes narrowed. "Did he, now?"

"So, did you get to the hotel for the keynote?"

"Yes. Daniel always does marvelous speeches." I detected a tinge of sarcasm in her voice as she whacked aside another clump of grass looking for her ball.

"It must be hard running a business together. I imagine it's not always easy on a relationship."

She eyed me then. It wasn't a friendly look. "I'm not sure what you are insinuating."

"I'm not insinuating anything. I've just always been curious about how couples handle business together."

She sighed. "It's not easy, that's for sure. Especially when only one of us knows how to run a company."

I was surprised that she offered that information so freely. Maybe she had no one to talk to about it and I seemed like a faceless entity that she might never see again, not unlike a bartender at some two-bit hotel bar.

"Yes, I can imagine that trust is probably the biggest thing you need in a business." I knew something about that, especially as Jeremy had betrayed me, had betrayed my trust. It was on the same level as a betrayal in a marriage or a relationship. Trust was something I valued because I'd had a couple of other disastrous relationships, too.

Pamela looked at me and nodded. "That's very true."

There was a glint in her eyes that told me she knew something about betrayal, too. Did she know or suspect that her husband was having an affair? If she didn't, I wouldn't be the one to tell her. It wasn't my place or my business. The last thing she'd want to hear from a stranger was that her husband was having an affair with a younger woman.

I watched her hobble over to another clump of grass and swat at it. "If your leg is bothering you, I can go get the cart," I offered.

She shook her head. "I'm fine. It's an old injury. I usually have my cane, but I forgot it in the rush to get here."

"Oh, that's a shame."

Deciding that it was wrong of me to continue to pump her for information, I discreetly lifted my foot off her ball and nudged it to the side. I then made a motion with my club on the grass, as if I had just discovered it.

"Oh, look. I found it. You can't play it from here." I picked the ball up and handed it to her.

When she took the ball from my palm, I had the distinct feeling that she'd known I'd been stepping on it the whole time. Maybe she needed the reprieve from the hustle and bustle of the conference.

Without another word, she set the ball down on the grass at the edge of the tree line, lined up her club, and knocked the ball out onto the green where Justin and Daniel waited for us.

CHAPTER TWENTY-FIVE

WHEN WE FINISHED THE nine holes, we met up with everyone in the clubhouse. Daniel and I had both ended up with two under par. I liked that it didn't seem to bother him that I had scored as well as he did. A lot of men took their sports too seriously and hated when women bested them. Jeremy had been like that. The one time I had beaten him when we were playing with clients, he had pouted like a child. Next time we played, I'd made sure to hold back.

Daniel bought us a round of drinks. I opted for a tall glass of ice water. I still had a headache from the whiskey. As we all cheered for a round well played, Pamela's husband Steve joined us. He kissed his wife dutifully on the cheek then smiled at me. She wrapped her hands around his arm, more for support, I think, than anything else.

"So, how did everyone fair?"

"Andi here was our little star player," Pamela said.

"Really?" Steve lifted an eyebrow.

"Why does everyone seem so surprised?"

Steve looked me over. "I guess you just don't seem like someone who plays golf well."

I had a sense that he meant I didn't look wealthy enough to play the sport well. The Bowers were the type that respected money and power and not much else.

"Andi used to play with big-shot lawyers in California," Daniel said with a grin.

"You're a lawyer?" Steve asked.

Before I could answer, Daniel said, "She used to work for one of the biggest firms in California. From what I heard, she was their most hardworking and diligent associate."

I narrowed my eyes at Daniel. Then I grabbed his arm and pulled him to the side. "Did you investigate me?"

"I always like to know who I'm dealing with."

"I didn't realize we had any dealings together."

He smiled. "Not yet we don't." And with that, he walked away and started a conversation with another group of people.

I stared after him, wondering what the heck that meant. As my gaze roamed the clubhouse, it fell on a tall man with black hair in the corner near the door. He was staring right at me. He had a professional camera slung around his neck. The moment he saw that I noticed him, he ducked out.

I followed.

Outside the clubhouse, he lit up a cigarette and marched toward the parking lot. I ran to catch up to him.

"Hey."

He didn't stop.

"I'm talking to you."

He stopped and turned around. "What?"

"What are you doing here?"

"Taking pictures of the golf tournament for the hotel. What does it look like?"

"Are you Stan Zhang?"

"Maybe. What's it to you?" He blew his cigarette smoke into my face. I then noticed the filter on his cigarette. Marlboro.

Now, I knew well and good that lots of people smoked that brand. But I also knew when my instincts were calling out, loud and clear.

"Why have you been watching me?"

"I don't know what you're talking about." He turned to leave.

I didn't follow him; I didn't need to. I knew he'd been the one outside of my suite on the cliffs watching me. But why? Why would a private investigator be watching me? If he'd been hired to follow me, then I needed to find out by whom and why.

CHAPTER TWENTY-SIX

FOR THE NEXT FIFTEEN minutes, I milled about the crowd in the clubhouse, smiling and making niceties, and then made my escape. When I returned to my suite, Ginny was there directing two burly men who were fixing the balcony door. She was flirting with the one sporting a wild beard and a cheeky grin.

In response to my questioning look, she said, "I couldn't find Mick to fix the door. He's gone AWOL, and Lois is livid. So I had Jeff and Clinton come over. They own the hardware store in town."

I nodded to them both.

"How was it?"

"I finished two under par."

"That's pretty good. I should've warned you not to play well so that Lois wouldn't sign you up for more golf tournaments." She laughed. "But I know you would've played well regardless—you don't do anything halfway."

She was right. When I said I was going to do something, I did it to the best of my ability. In school, when the professor gave us a week to do something, I usually did it in two days, just because I could.

I went to the mini fridge and took out a bottle of water. I opened it, took a sip, and collapsed onto the sofa. Jem and Scout jumped on me, vying for my attention. They seemed a little bit upset about the intrusion into their lives, plus the loud pounding the men were doing to get the replacement door in place. I petted their little heads and was rewarded with happy purrs.

"Do you know the Bowers? Steve and Pamela?" I asked Ginny.

"Not personally. I know they own some big real estate development company. Why?"

"I golfed with Pamela. She's a bit of a cold fish."

"Not surprising. She's had to work hard for her position."

"What does that mean?"

"From the way I heard it, she basically came from nothing and worked her way into the Bower empire."

"Really? That's interesting."

She narrowed her eyes at me. "Andi? What are you thinking?"

I shrugged and took another sip of water. "Nothing. Just curious is all."

Ginny picked up Jem and cuddled her. "You are never *just* curious about anything."

I watched as the men finished up with the door, anxious to talk to Jeff. When I'd started talking about the Bowers, he'd perked up and even smirked when I'd mentioned Pamela being a cold fish. This was a small town on a small island; he probably had dealings with the Bowers in some capacity, considering he also worked in construction on the side.

As they packed up their tools, and Ginny leaned on the wall and flirted hard with Clinton, I handed a hammer to Jeff. He thanked me and put it into his toolbox.

"So, you must know the Bowers."

His eyes narrowed. "Why would you say that?"

"Because you're in construction and you reacted unfavorably when I was talking about Pamela Bower."

He smirked. "Yeah, she's a piece of work."

"How so?"

"I did a job for them a few months ago." He shook his head. "You shoulda heard her shouting at Steve. She was busting his balls about something."

"Maybe he deserved his balls being busted."

He nodded. "Probably. I hear the man has a hard time keeping it in his pants, if you know what I mean."

I nodded and said nothing, but I suspected that I did know exactly what he meant.

Chapter Twenty-Seven

AFTER THE CREW LEFT, and Ginny with them, still chatting up Clinton, I sat on the sofa and made the call I'd been dreading. Okay, so I knew it was really late in Hong Kong. I also knew my mother turned off her phone before she went to bed at night. Which meant I didn't expect her to answer. Call me a coward. I can live with that.

When the call bounced to voice mail, I took a deep breath and rushed through the upbeat message I'd practiced. "Hi, Mom and Dad. It's Andi. Just wanted to let you know that I've...moved. I'm on...hiatus from my job at the law firm, and I'm staying on Frontenac Island at the Park Hotel for a while. Hope you're both well. Talk later. Bye."

I disconnected, tossed the phone onto the sofa, and opened my laptop, prepared to do some digging into the Bowers. I yawned and stretched, realizing I hadn't had any decent sleep in days. I closed my laptop and thought about getting in a two-hour nap instead. Except I realized it was a prime opportunity right now to follow up with Steve Bower. He'd likely still be at the clubhouse.

I went down to the laundry to find Nancy first. Earlier, she'd given me all the information I needed to help her with the problem with her ex-husband. I hadn't had a chance to go over everything thoroughly, but I'd flipped through it enough to know that her ex didn't have a leg to stand on. She'd paid for the mortgage on the house, and he couldn't force her to sell it. I was hoping she'd be ecstatic enough about that outcome to do me another favor.

I ran into Megan at the machines.

"Do you know where Nancy is?"

"Up on the second floor, I think."

"Okay, thanks." I turned to go.

"Hey," she said, stopping me. "You didn't tell anyone about me and Patrick, did you?"

"No, of course not."

"Are you sure? Cuz my dad is acting all weird."

"Like I said before, I'm sure your dad wouldn't listen to me, anyway."

She snapped her gum. "Yeah, that's true. He says you're kind of annoying."

"Great."

I left the laundry and went in search of Nancy on the second floor. I found her with Tina cleaning a section of rooms. Nancy was making a bed when I peeked in.

"What's up?" she asked.

"I was hoping you could do me a favor."

"Did you go over my papers?"

"I did, and I have good news." I proceeded to tell her about how the law worked concerning matrimonial property and the monetary responsibilities of both parties. Basically, I told her she could tell her ex to shove the papers he sent her up his butt. She was very happy to hear that.

"What do you need?" she asked.

"Access to a room."

Ten minutes later, Nancy let me into Steve Bower's hotel room.

"You would not believe how fast this guy went through the mini bar." She shook her head. "Not sure how Pamela puts up with him."

"Do you know Pamela?"

She made a face. "Not personally, no. She's a bit younger than me, but my dad knew hers. They were both plumbers. She was just a regular girl from a regular blue-collar family. Then *bam* she marries the richest guy on the island."

As she talked, I went to the closet and opened it. Hanging inside was one of the spa robes. Beneath it was a pair of men's shoes. I picked one up and felt inside. It was slightly damp. I put it up to my nose and sniffed. There was a faint odor of chlorine mixed in with the other horrible smells. Also hanging up was a gray suit. That made sense considering everyone was wearing their golf attire for today's activities.

"Pamela used to be a champion swimmer, you know? Was heading to the Olympics but got injured. Car accident, I think."

I thought about her limp. "That's horrible."

"Yeah. It sucks." She waved her hand around the beautiful room. "But, hey, look at her now. She gets to stay in rooms like this, while I just clean them."

Nancy had to know that Pamela was not staying at the hotel, but I understood what she meant.

As Nancy wandered out, I looked over the rest of the room, searching for anything of consequence. I didn't find anything incriminating like an errant cell phone with lurid text messages or a pad of paper with clues written on it. I checked in the bathroom and found nothing but the usual toiletries for a wealthy man like Steve Bower and a pair of socks hanging over the towel rack. They smelled like chlorine.

I left the room, and Nancy closed up after me. I had to tell the sheriff about the robe and shoes before Steve could get rid of the evidence. Although I considered whether the items were really evidence of anything at all. Theoretically, Steve could've used the spa services just as Daniel had, and then came up to his room in the robe. But why were his shoes wet? Later I'd check with the spa to see if Steve had booked a service.

"Got what you needed?" Nancy asked.

I nodded. "Yeah, thanks." I was about to head for the stairs when another thought popped into my mind. I turned to her. "Ah, could I check out one more room?"

She sighed but didn't say no.

I went into Daniel's room quickly. I just needed to check on one thing. I opened the closet door and saw two suits hanging there. A charcoal-gray one, and the cobalt-blue one I'd seen him wearing the first day I met him. Relief washed over me, and smiling, I closed the door and left the room.

"Now, I'm done. Thanks."

I reached the door to the stairwell when I heard my name. I turned to see Lois walking toward me.

"What are you doing up here?" she asked.

"Ah, I was just giving Nancy some good news about her divorce."

She eyed me as if she was trying to decide if I was telling her the truth or not. Finally, she nodded.

"I heard you were a dynamo on the course this morning."

I shrugged. "I held my own."

"More than that, from what I heard. Mayor Evans couldn't stop raving about you." She narrowed her eyes at me. It was a warning. It screamed OFF LIMITS.

"It was…fun."

"So, I was hoping you'd do one more thing for me today."

I was just about to open my mouth and say, "But this is my day off," but I refrained. The tightrope I was balancing on was too wobbly right now. And thin. It was like standing on one toe on a strand of spaghetti.

"Sure," I said instead. "What do you need?"

"I need you to take a gift basket to Casey Cushing's mother. She's recovering at the hospital from hip surgery."

"Um, you want *me* to give a basket to the mother of the man whose job I've taken?"

She chuckled and shook her head. She patted me on the shoulder. "She's in room 306."

"Does Casey know who I am?"

"Oh yeah, he knows." She chuckled again. "Thanks, Andi. I really appreciate it."

CHAPTER TWENTY-EIGHT

THE BASKET WAS HUGE, so I couldn't carry it down to the village. I actually didn't even know where the hospital was. After asking Lane at the front desk and getting a map of the town, I pilfered a golf cart from the clubhouse and drove down the hill, the huge gift basket as my passenger. I passed Daniel, Lindsey, and Justin walking along the sidewalk. Daniel waved at me, a crooked, amused grin on his face. I waved back, trying hard not to blush from embarrassment.

Since I suspected the visit to the hospital was going to be awkward, I decided I needed some pick-me-up fuel, so I stopped at the café for an espresso. And an apple strudel. I had missed lunch again, and the strudel did have apples in it. So it was sort of nutritious and good for me. At least that was how I was selling it to my food-conscious brain. My stomach didn't care as long as there was something in there to digest for once.

After I was fully caffeinated, I returned to the cart, pleased no one had stolen my passenger, which I had almost forgotten about in my haste to get some coffee. I jumped in, started up, and was doing a U-turn to head down Main Street when I heard a woman cry out in distress nearby. I pulled over and noticed the very pregnant girl from the other night struggling with carrying a bunch of grocery bags up some stairs to an apartment above the corner pub. I parked and ran out to help her.

"Here," I said, trying to take the bags from her, "let me take these up for you."

"No, I got it." She held on to the bags. She was surprisingly strong.

"You shouldn't be carrying all this stuff in your condition, especially not up these steep stairs."

"I'm fine." But I could see the tears shimmering in her eyes. I knew it didn't all have to do with her groceries.

"You are clearly not fine." I tugged on the bags again. "I want to help."

"I don't want your help." She tugged back.

Now, the most logical thing to do in a situation like this would be to leave her to it and walk away. She'd said several times she didn't need my help. But not every problem could be solved with logic.

I looked her firm in the eyes and gritted my teeth. "I am helping you, whether you like it or not. I will not feel good about myself if I walk away from a very pregnant, upset young woman who needs help whether she knows it or not."

"Fine." She rolled her eyes but relinquished her grip on the grocery bags.

Carrying the bags, I followed her up the steep set of stairs. She unlocked the door and went in. I followed and set the bags in the tiny excuse of a kitchen. It was more like a kitchenette a person would see in a cheap motel off a long stretch of highway.

The rest of the apartment was clean, but it was small. I wondered how this girl was getting along. Did she have a job? Who was looking after her?

"Thank you," she said. "You did your duty. You can go now."

I nodded. I wouldn't push her. I could see she was on the edge of breaking. I didn't know what was going on, but I could certainly guess.

"Are you sure you don't need anything else?"

She shook her head.

"Okay. But I'm going to give you my number. My name is Andi, and if you ever need anything, please don't hesitate to call me." I turned and looked for some paper and a pen on the counter. I couldn't see anything except for a few non-descript envelopes, the kind bills or notices of overdue payments came in. That's when I noticed the name on the envelopes. I picked one up and turned to her.

"Sasha Wilkes."

She gave me a look. "Yeah, that's my name." She came toward me and snatched the envelope out of my hand. "Mind your own business."

"Is Thomas Banks your brother?"

Her eyes went wide, and she pressed her lips together. "I told you to go."

A million scenarios went through my head. None of them good. "Sasha, if you're in trouble, I can help you."

"Look, lady…I don't know what you think you know, but I don't need your help. Leave me the hell alone." She marched to the door, as best she could in her condition, opened it, and pointed for me to get out.

I couldn't leave. I just couldn't, not in good conscience. But I didn't know what else to do. She wanted me to go. I couldn't force her to take my help. Probably the best thing I could do for her, and for everyone, was to march over and tell Sheriff Jackson everything I knew and everything I suspected.

I walked to the door but stopped just before exiting. "I don't know why you're lying to me Sasha—you must have your reasons—but I want you to know that he's not worth it. He's not worth protecting. You need to think of your baby and what's best for it and for you."

Tears rolled down her flushed cheeks. She licked her lips, and I thought maybe she was going to trust me. Then her eyes went really wide, her mouth made a little O, and a rush of water splashed onto the floor and all over my second pair of new shoes.

CHAPTER TWENTY-NINE

"OH MY GOD, DID I just pee all over the floor?" Sasha sobbed.

"No, hun, your water just broke."

She shook her vehemently. "Nope. No way. I'm not due for another four weeks."

"Well, I'm thinking your baby doesn't care." I took her by the arm. "We should get you to the hospital."

"I don't want to go."

"You have to."

She rubbed a hand over her belly. "I'm not having contractions."

"Doesn't matter. When your water breaks, you risk the chance of infection."

"How do you know? Do you have kids?"

"No, I just read a lot." I pulled on her arm again, but she wasn't budging. "C'mon. I know you're scared, but it'll be all right. I promise."

"I'm not scared." She lifted her chin in defiance.

"Okay, but I am. I'd feel so much better if you were in the hospital, safely having this baby."

"Why do you care so much? You don't know me."

I sighed. "Because I found your brother's body, okay? That messes with a person. And I kind of feel obligated now to take care of his affairs. And I'm assuming he cared about you and would want you to be looked after."

She pressed her lips together. "I'll go get changed and get my bag." She disappeared into the bedroom and then returned in a pair of sweatpants and a baggy t-shirt. She slung a small, pink backpack over her shoulders. "Let's go."

I helped her lock up, then escorted her down the stairs to the golf cart. She looked at me funny when I nudged the gift basket over and told her to get in. "Don't ask," I said. "It's a long story."

Sasha guided me off of Main Street and onto Lilac Street that would take us right to the hospital. It was only six blocks away. Although I wasn't driving fast—the cart could only go twelve mph, fifteen if I pushed it—Sasha was hanging on for dear life. I wondered if her contractions had suddenly kicked in. I'd never been pregnant nor had a close friend who'd given birth, so I didn't really know how it all worked. I mean, I did from a biological standpoint, but not from reality.

"Are you okay?"

She nodded but didn't look at me.

"I'm really sorry about your brother."

"Thanks."

"I know you probably don't want to talk about it, but—" The cart sputtered and jerked, effectively cutting me off, until it rolled to a stop in the middle of the street. I glanced at the gas gauge. It was empty. I smacked the steering wheel with the heel of my hand. "Perfect."

"Did we just run out of gas?"

"Yes." I sighed. This was just how my week was going.

"It's only two blocks away. I can walk."

"Are you sure?"

She nodded and slid out of the cart.

I got out, grabbed the gift basket and her bag, after some back-and-forth tugging with her for a few minutes, then we started the short jaunt to the hospital. After walking half a block, Sasha stopped, put a hand on her belly, and grimaced.

"Oh crap," she groaned.

"Are you having contractions?"

She nodded and winced again, as I assumed another wave of pain surged over her.

I looked around. There was no one visible to help us. I looked up the street and could see the hospital. It wasn't far, but I was certain Sasha couldn't make it.

"Okay, I'm going to run to the hospital and get a wheelchair, then run back and get you."

She gave me a look like I was nuts. And I suspected she was right. I didn't really feel in control right now.

"You wait in the cart." I took her arm and helped her back to the cart so she could sit comfortably. Once she was seated, I hugged the gift basket tight and made a run for it. Anyone looking out the window would see some mad woman running by with a giant plastic-wrapped basket of sausage, crackers, and cheese.

CHAPTER THIRTY

I MADE IT TO the hospital, ran through the main doors, startling two elderly women and a nurse. "I need a wheelchair. My friend is in labor."

A nurse came out from behind the main counter, rolling one toward me. "Where is she?"

"About two blocks down that street."

"You left her there?"

"Well, I couldn't carry her, now could I?"

She stared pointedly at the huge gift basket in my arms and then rolled her eyes. She followed me down the two blocks to where I'd left Sasha. She was leaning forward in the cart and panting, using the breathing techniques that were universally taught for giving birth. The nurse helped her into the wheelchair, and we hightailed it to the hospital.

Once inside, the nurse wheeled Sasha to the right to take her to one of two maternity rooms. I followed along to make sure she got in there safe and sound.

Another nurse handed me a clipboard with a bunch of forms on it. "Could you please fill out your partner's information for me please?"

"Oh, we're not together."

She looked me up and down. "Uh-huh. Okay. Could you please fill out the forms? Thank you." And off she shuffled in her squeaky white shoes.

I carried the clipboard into the room, where the nurse was helping Sasha into a gown.

I immediately shielded my eyes and turned away. "Sorry."

Sasha responded with a vehement grunt of pain that made me cringe.

"I need to fill out these forms for you, Sasha. I'm just going to go into your purse to get your ID and such."

I set her bag down on the foldout chair and set the gift basket on the floor. Since she didn't oppose, I proceeded to unzip her bag and search around for her wallet. I took it out and flipped through it to find her ID. Using it, I filled out some of the forms. Then I went back to see if she had an insurance card. I didn't find any insurance, but I did find a strip of photos—like you get from those fun photo booths—of her and a man wearing sunglasses and a ball cap. They were kissing in two of the photos. Peering at them, I had the sense I recognized the man. It was hard to really tell with his eyes and hair covered. But he almost looked like Steve Bower. I wanted to ask Sasha about it but felt like maybe this was a really bad time to bring it up, considering she was just about ready to pop out a child. Maybe even Steve's child.

I put the photos back, then turned to find the nurse to give her the clipboard.

"I filled them out as best as I could."

The nurse took it and nodded. "Okay, Sasha. The doctor will be in soon to check to see how far along you are. The contractions are about seven minutes apart. So we're close, but it could still be hours yet before baby comes." She gave me a curt nod, then marched out of the room.

I watched as Sasha paced the room, bending over and wincing every once in a while. I was unsure of what to do. "Is there anyone I can call for you?"

She quickly shook her head.

"Any friends?"

Another shake of her head.

"Your mother maybe?"

"She's dead."

Way to step in it, Andi. "I'm sorry." I grimaced, remembering that I'd seen her mother's obituary during my research. "How about...the father?"

"Absolutely not."

"Um, okay, so...it looks like you're in good hands here, so I'm just going to go." I picked up the gift basket. "I need to deliver this basket, then—"

She cried out as she dropped to one knee.

Nearly tossing the basket aside, I rushed to her. "Are you okay?"

She cried out again.

After setting the basket onto the bed, I crouched next to her and patted her back. "It's going to be okay."

"No, I'm dying!"

"You're not dying, honey. You're having a baby." Pat. Pat. Pat.

She grabbed my arm and screamed. I swore she sounded just like the girl from the movie *The Exorcist*. I hated that movie.

Scared the bejeezus out of me. Gave me nightmares for years, just as I expected this whole event was going to as well.

Before I could do anything, the doctor and the nurse rushed into the room. The doctor was a pleasant-looking woman with pixie hair and a nose to match. She actually looked like a fairy. A tall, gangly fairy, mind you, but one nonetheless. She reached down and helped Sasha up to her feet, then shuffled her over to the bed.

"I'm Dr. Neumann, Sasha. I'll be your doctor. Now let's see what's going on down there."

While they maneuvered Sasha, and me by proxy, toward the bed, I tried to extract myself from the situation, but Sasha had a death grip on my hand. She was holding on like I was a life raft in a flood. The doctor got her settled with her legs up in stirrups and then got down to business.

"Looks like you're already dilated seven centimeters." She smiled at Sasha. "You're going to be having this baby very soon." She looked at me. "Are you her partner?"

I shook my head. "No, I'm Andi Steele. I'm the concierge at the Park Hotel."

Dr. Neumann made a face then chuckled. "Wow, you're really taking customer service to a whole new level."

"Yeah, you have no idea. Lois better give me a raise after this."

Sasha squeezed my hand so hard as she went through another contraction that I swore I could hear the bones break, then she let out a long string of curses in the guttural voice of the possessed. Curses that just about made me blush.

The doctor patted me on the shoulder. "I'll put in a good word for you with Lois. We play bridge together every Thursday night."

I couldn't respond through the tears streaming down my face thanks to the pain zinging up my arm. I tried to pry Sasha's fingers from my hand. "You're crushing me."

She screamed again, bowing her back, as another contraction hit her.

"Try rubbing her belly or shoulders. It'll help with the pain," the nurse suggested as she puttered around getting things together for the impending birth.

"What about *my* pain?" I grunted.

The nurse just chuckled. "Oh, you're lucky. The last birth we had in here, the husband got knocked on his butt from the mother's very well-placed uppercut. I don't think he saw it coming at all." She shook her head and continued to chuckle good-naturedly. "I totally did."

For the next four hours, I rubbed Sasha's belly, her shoulders, then her back, then her belly again. I coached her breathing, panting along with her, not caring that I made stupid faces while doing it. After the second hour, my stomach was grumbling so hard that I tore into the gift basket. I devoured an entire sleeve of vegetable crackers, a roll of sausage, and nearly a block of cheese. Thankfully there was some fruit and a bottle of Perrier water to wash it all down.

When the time was right, I urged Sasha to push, praising her with every advancement, and when the electricity of the room was finally punctuated with the robust cry of a tiny baby boy, I smiled and gently patted her on the shoulder.

"Well done," Dr. Neumann proclaimed. "He's a healthy little man." She gave Sasha's leg a gentle squeeze and then exited the room, having done her good work.

The nurse cleaned the little guy up, swaddled him tight, and set him into Sasha's arms. The nurse left the room. Even with her dark hair in complete disarray, sweat dotting her forehead and upper lip, her eyes glassy and a bit unfocused, Sasha was beaming with that new-mother glow.

"He's beautiful, Sasha," I said.

She nodded and pressed her lips to her baby's head. Tears dripped down her cheeks and kerplunked on his little face. He didn't seem to mind, though. He seemed quite content being out and proud and lying on his mom's chest.

"Is there anything I can get you?"

She pressed her lips together, and she seemed not far from completely breaking down. "Thank you for being here."

I smiled at her. "You're welcome. I couldn't leave even if I wanted to. You had a pretty good grip on my hand." I flexed it because it was still a bit stiff.

She bit down on her bottom lip, and I could tell she was struggling with something.

I put my hand on her shoulder and gave it a reassuring squeeze. "I'll make sure you get everything you need, Sasha. You don't need to worry. I'll figure something out."

She looked up at me. "Steve Bower is the father of my baby, and I'm pretty sure he killed my brother."

CHAPTER THIRTY-ONE

I GAPED AT HER, my mouth opening and closing like a guppy. "Okay," I said after I recovered. "Let's start with the first thing. You had an affair with Steve Bower?"

She nodded and nuzzled her face against her baby's head.

"For how long?"

"Almost a year."

"And I take it he broke up with you when you told him you were pregnant?" It was such a cliché, but it happened a lot. As a lawyer at a big firm with many wealthy clients, I'd been on the other side of that equation, trying to find ways to protect that client's money from situations like these. It had always been my least favorite part of the job.

"When I found out I was pregnant, I told him, and he told me we were through and that I couldn't prove the child was his."

"Does his wife know? About the affair?"

She shook her head. "No. Steve was adamant about that. He was scared that she'd divorce him and take the business and all the money. There was a prenup."

This confirmed what I'd been hearing around town. That Steve had all the assets and had provided all the initial income to start Bower Development. His family had amassed most of their fortune in the '70s and '80s from a well-known soap business. His parents were good friends with the families who started the company in the late '60s. Who knew cleaning products could be so lucrative?

I imagined Pamela had been forced to sign a prenup that protected all his money. But I imagined an affair and an illegitimate child on his part could make a lot of that contract null and void.

An affair was a scandal Steve literally couldn't afford.

I could probably infer how the affair had led to blackmail, which led to Thomas's death, but I needed to ask. I needed to be sure. Accusing someone of murder was extremely serious and couldn't be taken lightly.

"Why do you think Steve killed Thomas? Did he tell you?"

"I just know," she said.

"Do you have proof? Give me something I can take to the sheriff. If Steve killed your brother, he needs to be arrested."

She closed her eyes and breathed in her baby. There was something she didn't want to tell me. I didn't blame her. She was probably having a difficult time dealing with the fact that her baby's father may have murdered her brother. That wasn't an easy thing to digest. I'd have to pull the truth out of her bit by bit.

"Was your brother blackmailing Steve?"

She gave me a side-eye look around her baby's head, and I knew I had hit on something.

"Because of your affair and pregnancy?"

Before she could answer the nurse returned. "All right, time to get this little man fed, and time for him to bond with his mommy." She glanced at me. "Time for visitors to take a break and come back in a few hours after mommy and baby have gotten to know each other."

"I just need to talk to Sasha for a little bit—"

"Nope. Time for you to go." She said it with a smile, but she was all business. I admired nurses who could be both gentle as a lamb and as tough as a drill sergeant. They also scared me.

"Sasha, I will be back to make sure you're all right." I barely made it out of the room with the remains of the gift basket before the nurse shut the big, heavy door, missing my foot by mere inches.

As I stood there in the corridor, I considered my options. I could go to Sheriff Jackson with what Sasha had said, but I had no proof to back up her claims. If I was going to make accusations like murder and such about a prominent member of the town, I needed something to back me up. Otherwise, the sheriff would throw me out on my butt or, worse, harass Sasha about it. But first, I had to figure out what to do with the pitiful remains of the gift basket that I was supposed to have delivered already.

I'd eaten all the crackers, sausage, and gourmet cheese. Granted, I did share it with Sasha; she'd helped me devour the crackers. Giving birth was hungry business. All that was left was a teddy bear wearing a Get Well Soon t-shirt, an apple (I'd eaten both the pear and the orange) and some chocolate-covered almonds, which I was surprised I hadn't eaten. The cellophane had been ripped open and hung in tatters from the wicker basket. I couldn't present it as it was. I had to fix it up a bit.

As I made my way to the hospital lobby, I spied a gift shop/convenience store. I went inside and perused the shelves, looking for anything that could help fix the situation. I quickly grabbed a box of Ritz crackers, some pepperoni sticks, and a block of cheddar cheese I spotted in one of the refrigerated shelves next to the yogurt cups. I also snagged all the ribbon they had in the corner next to the get-well and sympathy cards. After paying for my purchases, I rearranged them all in the basket as best I could—I was definitely not a skilled basket decorator—then tore away the rest of the cellophane and tied all the ribbons around the basket handle. I nodded at my finished piece, satisfied, then took it and hurried down the other hallway looking for Mrs. Cushing's room. I was going to run in, drop it off, and get the heck out of there.

When I found her room, I slowly pushed open the door and peered in. There was an older woman in the bed, and she was sleeping. There didn't appear to be anyone else in the room. Perfect. I quickly walked in, making sure I was quiet. I set the basket down on the table beside her bed, then turned and was just about to march out, when the door to the adjoined bathroom opened. A tall young man with an artfully messy mop of blond hair and big brown eyes walked out.

He glanced at the basket, then at me. "Can I help you?" His voice was musical and cultured, with just a hint of a British accent. This had to be Casey Cushing. Everyone at the hotel, especially the ladies, had made a point of telling me how incredible he was.

"Ah, I just dropped off a gift basket from the Park Hotel."

He smiled, and I kid you not, the room actually lit up. "Oh, how nice. Lois and the whole crew are just so amazing to me."

I nodded. "Yeah, they sure are."

His eyes narrowed a little. "I don't think we've met before. I would definitely remember your face."

I had to tamp down the urge to girlishly giggle. The man was definitely blessed with high voltages of charm. "I'm Andi Steele."

"Ah, yes. Lois told me that she got someone to cover my job while I was taking care of my mom." He offered me his hand, and I shook it. His skin was exceptionally soft. "You're Ginny's old friend, aren't you?"

The way he said "old" made me think he was referring to my age and not that we were long-time friends, although he couldn't have been that much younger than me, maybe by seven years.

"Yes, Ginny and I went to college together."

"Oh, that's right, I heard you *were* a lawyer."

Oh, the joys of living in a small town. Everyone knew your business, even when you didn't want them to.

"Yeah. I'm just taking a much-needed break." I didn't know why I lied about my situation. Besides the fact that he didn't need to know the truth—it wasn't his business—I suddenly felt a whole surge of competitiveness with him. I wasn't someone who liked to lose. And I had a feeling that Casey Cushing had just set up the competition.

"Well then, I'm sure you'll be happy to move on once I'm able to return to work. It must be so boring here compared to the big city." He gave me a smile. I knew it was meant to win me over, but now that the gauntlet had been thrown down between us, it didn't do anything but piss me off.

"Well, we'll see. You never know what can happen in that time." I returned his smile. "Enjoy the basket." I then turned and left the room, happy that I had eaten most of the good stuff.

I left the hospital with a bit of a burn in my belly. And no, it wasn't food poisoning. It was the drive to do better, be better. I was going to be a better concierge than Casey Cushing. I just had to prove myself to Lois and to everyone at the hotel. And the best way to start was to figure out once and for all who killed Thomas Banks. I'd like to see Casey do that with his smarmy 100-watt smile and perfectly messy hair.

CHAPTER THIRTY-TWO

AS I APPROACHED THE golf cart, I realized it still needed gas. *Damn it.* I decided the easiest way to solve that problem would be to call Ginny and ask her to bring me a jerry can full of fuel. When I reached into my pocket for my phone, I felt something else in there. I pulled out a set of keys. At first I was confused as to what keys they were, and then I remembered that I'd helped Sasha lock up her apartment. During all the chaos, I'd forgotten about them.

As I looked at them in my hand, I thought about heading back to her hospital room and returning them, but then I thought that maybe she had proof somewhere back at her place about Thomas blackmailing Steve. That kind of information would be enough for the sheriff to launch a thorough look at Steven Bower.

My conscience poked at me a little, but I ignored it. If anyone caught me there, or asked, I'd just say I was there getting some things for Sasha and the baby. It wouldn't really be a lie, as I would definitely pack up some things for her while I was there anyway. Because of everything that had happened, what we'd experienced together, I felt a weird connection to Sasha. I wanted to help her in any way I could. I needed to help her.

I walked back to her apartment, making a mental note to call Ginny to help me get the golf cart back to the hotel before I got in too much trouble for taking it in the first place. Before I climbed the stairs, I made sure no one was around. I waited until a few loud tourists walked by, then I raced to the top, opened the door, and went inside.

She still had her phone with her, so I couldn't search that, but if she had a computer somewhere around…

I found a laptop in her bedroom and brought it out to the kitchen table. Little pieces of me felt bad about going through her stuff, but I had a killer to catch, and if anything here could prove motive or means, it was a risk I'd take. I'd apologize for it later.

I opened the lid and hoped the laptop wasn't password protected. I wasn't a hacker by any means and didn't know Sasha well enough to guess at what her password could be. I turned it on, and the generic ocean-themed screensaver filled the screen. I pumped my fist in the air. I was in! I clicked on her web browser, hoping she had bookmarks for all her regular internet doings. Most people did. We were a society that loved its conveniences. Yup, I spotted her banking, email, and most used search engine on the top toolbar.

I clicked on her email provider, knowing a lot of people saved their passwords in their computer. Again another dangerous convenience we used as a society. Like a million other people, I was able to access her emails with one click. I hated snooping through her private conversations, but it had to be done.

There was nothing glaring in her inbox. Just some emails from her bank and insurance company, probably checking up on some things for the impending birth of her son. She had some spam she hadn't deleted yet from retailers, a couple of dating sites, and the usual array of sexual advancements, marketing schemes, and Nigerian prince scams. I went through her sent emails but didn't find anything addressed to Thomas Banks, or T Banks, or anything obviously related to Thomas. Nothing directly related to Steve Bower, either. There were a couple of emails addressed to bowwow69, though.

I shook my head at the moniker. Some men just never grew up. I clicked on the first one and found an exchange between Sasha and someone who I assumed was Steve because it contained flirtatious wording about seeing each other and hooking up. The date on the last exchange was three months ago. So, if the recipient was Steve Bower, he and Sasha were still seeing each other when she would've been four months pregnant. There were no more emails between her and bowwow69 after that.

I continued the search through her sent folder and didn't find much of importance, except for a few emails to the Swan Song, which was one of the pubs on the island, about holiday pay and work hours. Sasha must have worked there at some point. The emails were dated seven months ago.

Nothing else popped out at me, so I clicked on her web browser. I checked her search history for anything interesting. Most recent searches were about pregnancy and all its relevant health information. She'd searched *warning signs of miscarriage* and the like a few times. Poor girl had obviously been alone and afraid for most of her pregnancy.

I continued to scroll down her search history. Seemed like Sasha rarely, if ever, deleted any of it. So stuff from months ago still showed up. I was just about ready to give up when a couple of search terms caught my attention. *Steve Bower* and *Bower Development*. The searches were made over a year ago. Before Sasha and Steve had started their affair, according to Sasha.

I clicked on the links. They took me to the Bower Development website and the bio of Steve Bower directly. I continued looking in the search history and found more searches: *Pamela Bower, Pamela Platt, Douglas Platt, places to rent on Frontenac Island, jobs on Frontenac Island, Swan Song.*

I sat back in the chair. I'd always assumed that Sasha was from here. But now I wondered if she had moved here only about a year and a half ago, after some research on Steve Bower. I didn't like where this was going.

I stared at her computer screen, and another icon caught my eye. I clicked on it. There weren't a lot of photos in it. For most people nowadays, photos were kept on our phones. I clicked on a folder, and several photos came up. I stared at them in disbelief. They were of Steve Bower. Leaving his house, driving to his office, coming home. There were others of Pamela and their kids, I assumed. Then there were a few of Steve out in the village. Going to the café, going to the store, and several of him going into and leaving a pub. The Swan Song.

Sasha had been casing Steve Bower. Their meeting and their affair hadn't occurred by chance—it had been orchestrated. From this, it certainly seemed like Steve Bower had been an unlucky mark.

Before I shut down the laptop, another photo file caught my eye. It was labeled "Zhang." I clicked on it, and several professional-looking photos popped up. There were a few pictures of Steve walking down Main Street. Him going around the corner, him mounting the stairs to Sasha's apartment. The door opening, Sasha allowing him to enter. There were two other photos obviously taken through the small window of her apartment. Sasha and Steve kissing, a shirtless Sasha straddling Steve on the sofa. The one I was sitting on right now.

And then the last two photos were of me. One of me standing outside of the hotel chatting with Ginny, and the other of me inside my suite, sitting on the sofa with my laptop on my lap and my two cats curled up beside me.

Chapter Thirty-three

AS I STARED AT the laptop screen, I tried to arrange all this new information in my mind, like putting together a puzzle. I hated the image that was forming. I wanted Sasha to be innocent in all this, but the truth seemed to be that she was complacent at best, an extortionist at worst.

Had she hired Stan Zhang to take the pictures? It would make sense if everything I'd found was all part of a blackmail package.

I took out my phone and typed in a list in my notes app. It would help me keep things straight when I went to see the sheriff and shared everything I'd found.

1. Sasha Wilkes is Thomas Banks's sister.
2. She has search information about Steve Bower on her laptop from almost two years ago.
3. She moved to the island shortly after that.
4. She took a job at pub Steve Bower frequented.

5. Had affair with Steve Bower re: emails on server with bowwow69.

6. Got pregnant.

7. Had Steve's baby.

I could've added other inferences, but I didn't have proof of the fact. The likely scenario was that she and her brother planned the con on Steve Bower. Pretty, sultry Sasha met Steve at a pub, flirted with him, etc., they started an affair, she got pregnant, then after Steve broke it off with her, I imagined the blackmail started by Thomas.

If that was all true, it was horrible for Sasha to purposely get pregnant and blackmail the father into giving her money. She could've sued Steve legally for child support. Unless getting pregnant hadn't been part of the plan.

Not to mention her claiming that Steve Bower killed her brother.

I had enough to take to Sheriff Jackson. It would give him plenty of reason to dig into Steve Bower and his financial records, and into his alibi. He could get proper warrants and enough evidence to prove the case. I took pictures of Sasha's laptop, open on the emails, and also took a picture of her search history.

My gaze then fell to the wooden baby cradle in the corner of the living room. I just didn't get why Sasha would do it. Had her brother coerced her into the plan? Why?

After putting her laptop back into her room, I packed a bag with clothes for Sasha, as well as the cute yellow onesie I found inside the cradle. Someone must've bought it for her. Thomas maybe? She didn't seem to have any friends around. Despite what she'd been involved in, I still felt sorry for her. With her brother dead, I didn't think she had anyone. Steve certainly wasn't going to be there for her.

I left her apartment and locked up. I would hit the sheriff's office first and then return to the hospital to drop off Sasha's things and to tell her what I had done. I didn't want Sheriff Jackson ambushing her, unprepared, while she was still in the hospital.

At the police station, the front desk was unoccupied, so I dinged the little bell on the counter. Deputy Shawn came out of the back, licking his fingers. He must've been having a late supper, as it was past seven o'clock now. My stomach also rumbled, the crackers, sausage, and cheese long forgotten.

"You're from the Park Hotel," he said with a slight tip of amusement to his lips.

"Guilty as charged."

"What can I do for you this evening?"

"I need to talk to Sheriff Jackson."

"He isn't here."

"He isn't here like last time when he was in his office and didn't want to be disturbed? Or he really isn't on the premises?" I motioned toward the closed blinds on the sheriff's office. From where I stood, I couldn't tell if there was a light on inside.

"He's not on the premises," he said. "Maybe I could help."

"Nope, it needs to be the sheriff. Do you know where I could find him?"

"No, sorry." He gave me a smile.

"So, if there was an emergency, you wouldn't be able to get in touch with him?"

"Is this an emergency?"

Damn it. He had me there. Was this an emergency? The information was really important...but emergency worthy?

"Okay, tell you what, call Sheriff Jackson, tell him Andi Steele has some information about the Banks murder and that he can call me on my cell phone." I took the pen and paper lying on the counter and wrote down my number, although I was pretty sure he already had it from when I gave him my statement after discovering the body. I slid the number to the deputy and left.

While I waited for his call—and knowing the sheriff, it might take a while—I decided to head back to the hospital and drop off the bag for Sasha. As I walked down Main Street to turn onto Lilac Street, I spotted the Swan Song pub across the street. Maybe I would just dash inside and find out when Sasha worked there and when she left. It would help my case that I was going to present to Sheriff Jackson.

I crossed the street and went inside. The place was in full swing, which didn't surprise me. It seemed the busiest places on the island were the pubs. Celtic music played, patrons laughed, glasses clinked as harried servers rushed around the room. I weaved my way around full tables and random drinking patrons to the bar to talk to the bartender, who was an older man with long gray hair to match his beard.

He smiled at me when I approached. "What's your poison, luv?"

"No poison. I was just wondering if you knew Sasha Wilkes."

His face scrunched up to think, then he shook his head. "Nope. Doesn't ring a bell."

"She used to work here, I think. Maybe six months ago?"

"Nope, sorry, luv. No Sasha has ever worked here."

"Are you sure? Maybe she worked other shifts, or maybe someone else hired her. She has long, curly dark hair, pretty."

He shook his head again. "I'm the owner and the manager. I do all the hiring. Never hired a Sasha. No girl on staff who looks like that. I'd definitely remember."

I nodded and left him a five-dollar tip, although I hadn't ordered a drink. "Okay, thanks." I left the pub and went out onto Main Street again.

I wasn't sure what that meant for my working blackmail theory. Sasha and Steve had obviously met somewhere else. But where? It couldn't have been somewhere random. She'd done her research. The meeting had to have been planned. I supposed I could just directly broach the subject with her.

I headed back to the hospital.

CHAPTER THIRTY-FOUR

I PASSED THE GOLF cart still parked on the side of the road. Thankfully, no one had stolen it. Lois would not be happy if that happened. I should probably do something about it before something did happen to it. I took out my phone and noticed I had a voice mail from my mother. Ugh. I couldn't deal with that issue at the moment. I called Ginny.

"Where are you? I thought you would've been back by now. You've been gone like seven hours."

"I know. It's a long story. Wondering if you can do me a big favor?"

"Sure."

"Could you come down to Lilac and," I peered at the other street sign, "Rose with a gas can? The cart I borrowed kind of ran out of gas."

Ginny snorted out a laugh.

"It's not really funny," I said.

"Yeah, it kind of is."

"Fine, it is. Can you come bail me out?"

"I'll be there in twenty minutes."

"Thanks, Ginny. If I'm not here, I'll just be at the hospital. I'll meet you back at the cart."

"Why are you going to the hospital?" she asked.

"It's part of that long story that I'll tell you about later." I ended the call and continued the walk to the hospital.

When I stepped through the front door and into the lobby, my phone buzzed from my purse. I thought it was maybe Ginny calling me back, or Lois calling to ask me what the heck was going on after getting an angry call from Casey Cushing about the state of the pathetic gift basket I'd dropped off, but it was—surprise, surprise—Sheriff Jackson calling me back in a timely manner.

"This better be good. You better have some real information to give me."

"Wow, have we really passed the polite greetings and introductions of our relationship and gone straight into the threatening, bullying part already? I thought that would've been after at least a month of aggravating each other."

He sighed loudly and then spoke slowly, with a clipped cadence. I almost smiled at how much I'd gotten under his skin. Okay, who was I kidding? I was grinning like a Cheshire cat with a whole lovely bowl of cream.

"Hello, Ms. Steele. It's Sheriff Jackson."

"Hello, Sheriff. Thank you for calling me."

"What do you have?"

I guess one sentence worth of politeness was all I was going to get out of him. I supposed I should take small victories when they are offered.

"I met a woman named Sasha Wilkes. She's Thomas Banks's sister, and she just had a baby. Steve Bower's baby." I thought about telling him about Sasha's claims that Steve killed her brother, but I didn't have any proof and that was a serious accusation to make about someone, so I decided to just give him the blackmail angle, and he could connect the evidence and build a case as such.

"I'm pretty sure Sasha and her brother Thomas were blackmailing Steve Bower about the affair."

There was silence on the other end of the phone.

"Hello? Sheriff? Are you still there?"

"Yeah, I'm here."

"Did you hear what I just said?"

"Oh yeah, I heard. You're telling me Steve Bower is involved in the murder of Thomas Banks."

"Well, technically, I didn't say that. I'm saying that Steve Bower had an affair with Sasha Wilkes, Thomas Banks's sister. Where that leads is up to you."

"Well, I just had a conversation with Steve Bower here at the hotel, and he's telling me that you've been harassing him, and you've been unlawfully in his hotel room."

"What? That's preposterous."

"You haven't been in his hotel room without his permission or knowledge?"

I chewed on my bottom lip. How did he find out? I didn't think Nancy would tell him the truth, just the backstory we'd created together. "Well, I did go into his room, but I had a complaint that the carpet outside his room was wet. I thought maybe there was a leak inside or something. It had to be checked on."

"By the concierge? Doesn't maintenance handle that kind of stuff?"

"Technically, yes, but the maintenance guy wasn't on site." I grimaced at the lie. Although I was pretty sure the maintenance

202 | DIANE CAPRI

guy wasn't at the hotel when I decided to riffle through Steve's room, because he wasn't available to handle installing a new balcony door in my suite.

"Who else's room did you go into to inspect *a possible leak*?"

"No one's." He didn't need to know that I also went into Daniel's room to confirm that his cobalt-blue suit was hanging up in the closet. It was.

"Where are you?"

"I'm at the hospital."

"Stay there. I'm on my way, and we're going to have a long conversation."

"Fine. Good. Then you can talk to Sasha Wilkes, and she can tell—"

He ended the call before I could finish.

I slid my phone back into my purse and marched down the corridor to the maternity rooms. I knocked on the closed door to the second room, opened it, and peered inside. "Sasha? It's just me, Andi."

But the room was empty.

I walked in and looked around. The bed was neatly made, and there was no sign of her, baby, or her pink backpack. I returned to the reception desk and talked to the nurse there.

"Sasha Wilkes. The woman who just gave birth. Do you know where she is?"

The nurse smiled at me. "She went home."

"Are you sure?"

"Oh, yes."

"Did she leave on her own?" I didn't know how she could have without me seeing her walking back to her apartment.

"No, she had a friend with her. She came with a baby seat for the baby and helped Sasha carry the little guy out to the car. She said she was taking them to the home by the sea. Isn't that sweet?"

"Do you remember what this friend looked like?"

The nurse gave me a look, like I was asking her a complicated math problem. "She had blond hair. Smart dresser. Oh, and she walked with a cane." She gave me another smile and went back to her computer.

My stomach lurched into my throat. There was only one person I knew who looked like that. Only one person I knew who would have an interest in Sasha Wilkes and her baby. Pamela Bower.

CHAPTER THIRTY-FIVE

WHILE I WAITED AT the hospital for the sheriff to show up, I texted Ginny to tell her it would be a bit before I could meet her at the cart, then I paced the main lobby, like a captive lion I once saw in the zoo. I'd felt sorry for that animal. I knew it wanted to hunt down all the people who were outside the cage and rip their throats out. Not that I *necessarily* felt that way about the nurses and patients waiting to be admitted who looked at me like I was a bit off.

I took another sip of the strong hospital coffee I managed to commandeer from one of the staff rooms. I'd been looking for the washroom and stumbled inside. No, that wasn't true. I went in there purposely to find some caffeine. No one had caught me, so…no big deal.

I couldn't figure out why Pamela had come to pick up Sasha. How did she even know she was here and that she had the baby? How did she even know who Sasha was? Why would a woman seek out her husband's mistress and befriend her? I was missing something. There was a piece of the complicated puzzle that I hadn't yet found or couldn't see.

The second Sheriff Jackson walked through the sliding glass doors, I pounced on him.

"Sasha's in danger. What are we going to do?"

He put his hand up as if to ward me away. "First off, how do we know this woman is the victim's sister? I didn't find anything about his next of kin."

"I found an obituary notice for Helen Banks, who was his mother, and it listed Thomas and Sasha as her children. I did a search for a Sasha Banks but didn't find her anywhere. It was actually purely accidentally that I found her here, living on the island under a different name—Sasha Wilkes."

He sighed, took off his hat, and ran a hand through his hair. "Okay, tell me everything you got."

I prattled off all the information I had gleaned over the past few days about Sasha and Steve Bower, and my main working theory. Although Pamela's sudden appearance at the hospital did give my speculation a bit of a spin.

"So, I'm thinking Pamela has either found out about Sasha and the baby and is maybe exacting her revenge, or she's been in on the whole thing from the start."

"Do you really think Pamela Bower would hurt this woman and her baby?"

I shrugged. "I don't know. You know her better than I do. I've only been on the island for a week. She has kids, so maybe she wouldn't hurt the little boy, but the woman who was having an affair with her husband? I'm thinking she's fair game."

I could tell he was pondering something by the way he literally chewed on the inside of his cheek. The muscles along his square jaw flexed.

"I'm onto something, aren't I?"

"Her kids are adopted," he said. "The word around town was she couldn't get pregnant, although they tried for a lot of years. Steve supposedly hadn't wanted to adopt."

Well, *damn*, small-town gossip was brutal. I could just imagine what the rumor mill had already concocted about me. Maybe Ginny would fill me in later. Although my nanny always said to me, "Someone's opinion of you is frankly none of your business." That might've been good advice.

"Do you have a picture of this Sasha Wilkes?"

I took out my phone and showed him a picture I had discreetly taken of her in the golf cart.

His eyes narrowed. "She looks familiar."

"Does she?" I looked at the photo with renewed interest. "I thought she had worked at the Swan Song pub and that's where she met Steve, but I went over there, and the owner said he didn't know her."

"I've seen her before," he said, "but can't quite place where."

"Well, regardless, I still think she's in danger. We need to find her."

"I will find her. What you need to do is go back to the hotel and stay there."

I gave him a look. "After all the evidence I've given you? You wouldn't have a clue without me."

"Well, since you're calling me out, I will let you in on a little secret. Steve Bower was already on our suspect list. We managed to trace money going into Thomas's bank account from the Bowers' development company. We also found a burner phone in his car that had texts from the victim on them."

I gave him a smug smile, I couldn't help myself. "I'm happy that you took my advice and followed the money."

208 | Diane Capri

He shook his head. "There's no point in correcting you on that, is there? No point in telling you how a proper investigation is conducted, and how there is a way of doing things that don't involve going off half-cocked, running around the island thinking you're Magnum PI."

"No, probably not."

"I didn't think so."

"If you are so on top of it, why haven't you issued a warrant for Steve Bower's arrest yet?"

He gave me a look. "Who says I haven't?"

"Oh," I said, not wanting to eat crow. "Well done, then."

"What were you looking for in his hotel room, anyway?"

"The spa robe. The one he would've worn after stashing his suit in the shower drain."

"And was it there?"

I nodded. "Oh yeah. I also found some socks drying out in the bathroom. I bet if you tested them, you'd find chlorine on them."

"Good to know. Thanks."

I smiled. "Wow, you actually showed me some gratitude. I'm stunned."

"Don't get used to it." I may have been seeing things, but I swore I saw his lips twitch up inside of down. "Now, go home. I will locate Pamela Bower and Sasha Wilkes and her baby."

"Go easy on Sasha, okay? She may have been part of Thomas's blackmail scheme, but she's a good girl. That baby has no one but her."

"Noted." He tipped his hat to me, then left the hospital.

CHAPTER THIRTY-SIX

I MADE MY WAY back to the stranded golf cart. Ginny was there waiting patiently for me. The minute she spotted me, she jumped out of her cart. "Oh my God, did you hear? Sheriff Jackson is going to arrest Steve Bower for that guy's murder."

"Wow, is there nothing that's secret in this town?"

She shrugged. "Not really."

"I'll have to keep that in mind."

"You must be so relieved that it's going to be all over soon," she said.

"I am." It was true, but there was still this niggling of doubt bothering me. Like when something gets stuck between your teeth and you keep touching it with your tongue. That was me with the fact that Pamela and Sasha knew each other.

I grabbed the jerry can from Ginny and filled up the tank on my cart. It was way past time I got back to the hotel and finally got some rest. I was starting to crash and burn. The end result wouldn't be pretty.

"Oh hey, look." Ginny showed me her phone screen. "You're famous."

I took the phone from her and saw my photo, one of me golfing. It was from the fifth tee when I'd smacked that ball and nearly got a hole in one. Despite how tired I'd been that morning, I thought I looked pretty good. My legs at least looked trim and shapely.

"Where's this photo?"

"The hotel's web page. We always have pictures from all the events on here."

As I stared at my photo, I remembered flipping through the photos on the Park Hotel's page when I was looking for one of Lonnie Morehead. That event had been last year's Flower Festival. I tapped on the screen to access all the photos. I went to the Flower Festival album and started scrolling through the pictures. I remembered seeing a couple of Steve and Pamela Bower on there. I found the one I was thinking of and zoomed in on it.

Between the two Bowers was another woman. A young woman with long, curly dark hair. Pamela had her arm around her, and they were both smiling. It was Sasha Wilkes. Under the picture was the caption: *The Bower Development Team*. Sasha had worked for the Bowers—that was how she and Steve had met. Pamela had to have known about their affair. Why didn't she do something about it? Unless...

She was the one who set it up.

"Holy crap."

Ginny grabbed her phone. "What? The picture's not bad. You look pretty good, I think."

"It's not my picture," I said. "Do you know where the Bowers are building houses?"

She frowned. "What? Why?"

"Do you know?" I must've given her a hard glare because she frowned even deeper.

"They have a few housing developments around here and on the mainland, I'm pretty sure." She tapped on her phone. "I can look them up."

"Is there one by the water? Maybe called By the Sea or something like that?"

"Hmm, there's one on the other side of the island called Eden Beach?"

"That's got to be it." I jumped into my golf cart. "Do you know where it is?"

She put her hand on her hip and gave me an inquisitive look. "What's going on? And don't lie to me, Andi Steele. I know all your tells."

I sighed. "Well…"

"You don't think Steve Bower did it."

"I don't not think that. I just think there's more going on, and I think Sasha Wilkes, the woman I helped have a baby today, may be in some trouble."

She walked around my cart and slid into the passenger's seat. "I'll get the guys to come down later and collect my cart. I'll direct you."

"Are you sure? I don't want to drag you into this."

"Hey, Batman always needs Robin."

I made a face. "Could you do a different reference? I'm not a big comic book fan, to be honest."

She shook her head. "Just drive, Sherlock."

Chapter Thirty-seven

GINNY DIRECTED US OUT of town and down the shore of the lake to a new housing development being constructed by the Bowers. There was a big sign, *Welcome to Eden Beach*, as we passed twin stone pillars that formed the "gate" to the new subdivision. As we drove down the darkened road, there were a couple of streetlamps glowing—Victorian, like those at the hotel—and two houses that had lights on inside. I assumed Pamela, Sasha, and the baby were in one of them. I parked the cart right before the first house.

"So, what's the plan, here?" Ginny asked. There was a slight waver to her voice. I didn't know if it was because she was cold or a little afraid. I, in fact, was a bit of both. An open golf cart gave no reprieve from cool lake air.

"I don't know, honestly."

"Andi, we should just call the sheriff and let him handle it."

"Okay, but I just want to make sure that Sasha is here and that she and the baby are safe." I jumped out of the cart before

Ginny could protest, as I knew she would, and ran across the yard to the first house. I flattened myself against the side wall and peered into the large living room window.

Thankfully, there were no blinds or curtains covering the window, so the room was clearly visible; I could also see part of the kitchen. The house was furnished with high-end pieces, but it didn't look "lived-in." There were no magazines or books on the side tables, or cozy blankets thrown over the sofa. No remote lying on a cushion or on the coffee table readily accessible for an evening of television. It was not how a normal home would appear. This must've been one of the show homes for the new area, where everything was clean and organized and fake.

I waited for another few minutes to see if there was any movement in the house. Everything remained still and quiet. I glanced over my shoulder to check on Ginny. She was still sitting in the cart, her hands gripping the steering wheel hard, ready to make a speedy getaway if we needed to. I decided to check out the second house.

I dashed across the expanse of lawn between the two estates and plastered myself up against the wall. Slowly, I moved along until I could easily peer through the side window into the living room. After a minute or two, I thought I'd made a mistake, but a shadow of movement flitted by the sofa. Getting my face even closer to the glass, I could see the baby in a carrier on the floor near the coffee table. For now, he seemed safe.

I took out my phone and called the sheriff. He answered almost immediately. "You're calling me from the hotel, right?"

I put my hand up over my mouth to talk. "I'm at the Eden Beach housing development. I can see the baby inside one of the houses. I'm sure Sasha and Pamela are here, too."

"You're what? I didn't catch that."

"Eden Beach. Get your butt here—"

From inside the house, the sound of shattering glass permeated the heavy silence, sending a wave of goose bumps up my back and down my arms. My hands flinched, and I dropped my phone onto the cement. The screen spider-webbed into a hundred fragments. I picked it up and tried to turn it on, but it was dead.

CHAPTER THIRTY-EIGHT

WITHOUT THINKING, I RUSHED to the front door and tried the knob. It was locked.

"What's going on? Is everything okay?"

I jumped, my heart leaping into my throat. I whipped around to find Ginny had crept up on me and was now standing on the bottom porch step, eyes wide.

"Call the sheriff, tell him it's an emergency. I can't. My phone's broken." Then I stepped off the front porch and ran around to the back of the house. There had to be another way in. Ginny followed me.

"I'm coming, too," she loud-whispered.

"Call the sheriff," I loud-whispered back.

"I'll text him." She quickly typed up an emergency text. "Damn it, I can't get service."

I crept onto the balcony, still trying to stay to the shadows. Through the big windows, I could see Sasha sweeping up glass shards from the counter and into the trash bin. I was relieved to see it was just a glass that had broken and nothing more ominous. The screen door was open a crack.

I turned to Ginny. "You stay here. I'm going inside."

She grabbed my arm. "Let's wait for the sheriff."

"I'm not sure he's coming," I said. "And I need to make sure Sasha and the baby are safe. You keep trying to call him. Go back toward the road to see if you can get a signal."

She let go of my arm, and I shuffled closer to the door. I slid it open and stepped inside the kitchen. Sasha looked up, a surprised O on her face. She did a quick glance over to the living room.

"What are you doing here?" she asked, her voice low and controlled.

"I wanted to make sure you were okay. When I heard Pamela Bower picked you up, I became concerned."

"I'm fine." Another glance over her shoulder. "You should go."

"Steve's being arrested for your brother's murder, did you know that?"

She nodded. "He deserves it. He killed Thomas." Then she grabbed my arm and started nudging me back toward the open screen door. "You should go, Andi."

"Pamela hired you to work at the company, didn't she? And the major part of your job was to seduce Steve?"

She didn't say anything, but the look on her face told me the answer.

"She was going to give you a big payout once she divorced, right? His affair would've broken the prenup. Pamela could take him for everything now. It would definitely set you up for a while." I frowned, trying to put all the pieces together. "Your pregnancy was a mistake, though. That wasn't supposed to happen."

Sasha chewed on her bottom lip, and she was close to tears. "Anthony is not a mistake."

"How did Thomas fit into all of this? That I can't quite figure out. If you are getting all that money from a divorce settlement, why the blackmail?"

Pamela limped into the kitchen, leaning heavily on a cane. "Hello, Andi."

Chapter Thirty-nine

"YOU DON'T SEEM TOO surprised to see me."

Pamela smiled, but it was cold. A shiver ran down my back. "I knew you'd get here eventually," she said. "You've been snooping around long enough."

"Sheriff Jackson is on his way." I figured the little white lie was in order. Honestly, he could be on his way. He might've heard and understood my last message before I dropped and broke my phone.

She arched a brutally sculpted eyebrow at me. "I have nothing to hide."

"You paid Sasha to seduce your husband."

"Between you and me, it's not illegal. Private investigative firms do it all the time," she said. "Besides that, she worked for Bower Development and was paid regular wages. There's nothing untoward about that."

I turned toward Sasha. "Why are you trusting her?"

"Pamela is helping me out." Her voice wasn't that steady. I didn't think she was too secure in her decision.

Pamela took a step toward Sasha, her cane tapping on the kitchen tile. "That's right. Sasha is a former employee that I saw needed a hand, so I'm doing that for her."

I regarded them both; this was not the pretty picture they were trying to paint. There was something wrong here. I could see it in the way Sasha fidgeted and rubbed her hands together. She was nervous. If Pamela were truly a friend in all of this, Sasha wouldn't look like she was about to jump out of her skin.

Pamela tilted her head and smiled at me. "There's nothing nefarious going on here, Andi. I'm helping out a new mother. I'm known for my charitable acts." She put her arm around Sasha's shoulders. "Sasha is naturally grieving the horrible loss of her brother, by her ex-lover no less. I mean the fact that Steve smashed Thomas's head in…it's unconscionable. I hope he rots in jail for a long time. I don't want a murderer around my children."

I frowned as I watched her. She moved her head again, and the light in the kitchen glinted off her gold earrings. I stared at her ears. I'd seen those type of earrings before. In the pocket of Steve's suit jacket that had been stuffed into the drain in the spa.

"How did you know Thomas had been hit in the head?"

She shrugged. "It must've been in the paper or on the news."

"It wasn't. Sheriff Jackson suppressed that information. Only a few people knew that was the cause of death. The sheriff, the medical examiner, me, because I read the autopsy report, and…well, the killer."

Sasha's head snapped to the side to look at Pamela. "What is she talking about?"

"Nothing." She sniffed derisively. "Andi is just grasping at straws. She's trying to prove that she's still some hotshot lawyer

from California, instead of just a simple hotel concierge."
Pamela glared at me as she came around the kitchen island, the
tapping of her cane echoing through the silence in the empty
house. "I think you have overstayed your welcome here. It's time
for you to leave." She pointed her cane at the sliding door I had
just come through.

My gaze went to her polished wooden walking cane. The
brass handle was curved, one end blunted, the other came to a
point. A point that could quite easily, with enough force, make
quite an indent in someone's temple. The medical examiner
reported a wound just like that in his preliminary report.

"Steve didn't kill Thomas."

She frowned, the lines on her forehead deep. "Of course he
did. All the evidence points to it."

"Evidence you planted. Steve's suit stuffed in a drain, the
spa robe in the closet in his hotel room, the socks. What you
didn't realize, though, is that there was an earring in his pants
pocket. Just like the earrings you're wearing now. In fact, they
are identical. What'd you do? Buy another pair?"

"Don't be ridiculous," she spat. The small veins along her
temples and neck flared.

During our little conversation, Sasha had started to back up
out of the kitchen. Her face was a mask of fear. I didn't blame
her. I looked at her. "Sasha, get your baby, and get out of
here."

"Don't you move, you little whore." Pamela turned toward
her, her one hand twisting on the handle of her cane, the other
clenching into a fist. "After all I've done for you. You'd still be
on the street if it wasn't for me."

I didn't like the menacing look on Pamela's face, so I
stepped forward, putting myself between her and Sasha. I put my

hand out toward Pamela. "Maybe it was an accident, and you never meant to kill him."

"He got in the way. He shouldn't have taken it upon himself to blackmail Steve. It was stupid."

"You killed Tommy?" Sasha pushed past me to advance on Pamela.

Pamela took a step back and slid her hand down the length of her cane. I shoved Sasha into the kitchen counter just as Pamela swung the stick like a baseball player at bat. I ducked just in time. The end smashed the two glasses on the counter, sending tiny glass fragments like missiles through the air. The sting was instant as a tiny fragment grazed my cheek.

All the commotion woke the baby, and he started to wail. I grabbed Sasha and pushed her toward the living room. "Get him and get out!"

Pamela swung her cane again at Sasha as she scrambled over the broken glass on the floor and out of the kitchen. The woman was wild with rage. Her face was contorted and beet red. She hit the counter this time, and it rattled her, knocking her a bit off balance.

Using this to my advantage, I swiveled and rushed her before she could swing that thing again and clock me in the head with the pointy end. I wrapped my arms around her, trapping one of hers to her torso and took her down to the ground. The cane clattered onto the floor as we landed on the hard tile with a thud and a groan. I knocked one of my knees on the metal leg of one of the island stools. Pain zipped up my leg like electricity. The takedown move looked so much easier online.

Pamela tried to shove me off, but I still had a solid hold on her. When that didn't work, she yanked on my hair and raked her fingernails over my face.

"Yow! That hurt!"

"Good," she growled, then yanked even harder on my hair and rolled me onto my back so she could straddle me. I tried to buck her off, but her legs crushed me to the floor.

She reached for her cane, grabbed it, and raised it above her head over me. The maniacal look in her eyes made my blood run cold. I lifted my arms and crossed them over my head to block the swing. Squeezing my eyes shut, I braced for the blow.

"Andi!" It was Ginny's voice.

I opened my eyes just as Sheriff Jackson dragged Pamela Bower off me.

Ginny rushed to my side, her hands pawing at my head and face. "Oh God, are you okay? Where are you hurt?"

"My face," I grunted. "Which you need to stop touching."

"Right, sorry." She helped me to my feet.

Sheriff Jackson was putting handcuffs on Pamela. "You are under arrest for assault."

"She killed Thomas Banks as well," I offered. "And planted all the evidence…"

Sheriff Jackson gave me that look of his. The one that said, *Shut up. Now.*

"You have the right to remain silent. Anything you say can and will be used against you in a court of law. You have the right to have an attorney." He glanced over at me briefly. I wondered if he thought I was going to offer to be hers or something. As if. "If you cannot afford one, one will be appointed for you by the court. Do you understand these rights?"

She gave a barely discernable nod before she was handed over to Deputy Shawn, who took her out of the house. The sheriff walked over to me, his eyes rooted on my face.

I pointed to the cane that was on the floor by my foot. "That's the murder weapon. She likely cleaned it, but I imagine you'll find traces of blood on it. Luminol will probably work."

His gaze didn't falter. "Are you okay?"

"Oh yeah, I'm good." I wasn't. My cheek throbbed like it was on fire and so did my scalp. I pretended I hadn't seen a chunk of my hair in Pamela's hand when the sheriff pulled her off me. I was afraid to put my fingers up in there in case I felt bone and/or blood.

He gripped my chin with his fingers and turned my face this way and that. "You won't need stitches." His hand dropped, and he rubbed the palm along the side of his jeans. I wondered if he was rubbing off my blood.

"Well, that's something, I guess."

"I thought I told you to go back to the hotel."

I shrugged, and even that hurt. "You should know by now I'm no good at listening."

"Well, definitely not to me, anyway."

I laughed, I couldn't contain it. I figured it was probably better than the sob I kind of wanted to let loose. And not a sad sob, but an angry, frustrated, I-just-got-my-butt-kicked kind of emotional release. I figured it had been building since the moment I left the conference room at my old law firm after the partners kicked me out of the only career I'd ever really wanted.

He looked me over one more time and then nodded. "Take her home, Ginny, and patch her up." He turned as Deputy Shawn came back into the house. "Shawn, bag this and tag it." He pointed to the cane on the floor.

Ginny put her arm around me and started to lead me out of the house.

"Wait." I swirled around. "What about Sasha? Will she be okay?"

He nodded. "I'll make sure she's looked after. She'll be interviewed, but I don't think there's anything to indicate she had anything to do with her brother's death."

"Okay. Thanks." We continued to the door, but I stopped again. "Call me when she's free to go."

"I will."

"You better."

He shook his head and turned around to finish collecting any other evidence in the house.

Ginny led me back to the golf cart. She wrapped a heavy jeans jacket around me after I slid into the passenger's seat. I don't know where she'd gotten it from, but it had just a tinge of citrus, something like the Old Spice aftershave Henry Park always wore, and all the scents belonging to a man. I had a feeling the coat belonged to Sheriff Jackson. The scent reminded me of him. A bit rough, but with just a hint of vanilla at the center. It was surprising, but not all that unpleasant. Go figure.

CHAPTER FORTY

WHEN GINNY GOT ME back to the hotel, she escorted me to my suite and proceeded to doctor me up, which consisted of excruciatingly painful astringent to disinfect the cut and scratches on my cheek, then the attaching of a Hello Kitty bandage to my wound. She offered to check my head, but I decided I didn't really want to know right at that moment how much hair I'd lost in the fight. She assured me there was no bald spot. But the way her pert little nose crinkled when she said it, I didn't think she was being entirely truthful. I guess nothing but a good mirror would confirm. Just not right now.

She suggested I have a long hot bath to ease some of the stiffness I was sure to feel later, but instead I shuffled up to my bed, pulled back the covers, and climbed in. A week of exhaustion had caught up to me. The second my head hit the pillow, I was out.

Later, Ginny told me that I had mumbled in my sleep, barking out orders to Sheriff Jackson, and that Jem and Scout had curled up around my head and stayed with me the entire night, alternating grooming styles. Jem would lick my face, and Scout would knead my hair. I guess Ginny had stayed with me as well, falling asleep on the sofa and then getting up at ten o'clock to go take care of some business. She told me I hadn't moved a muscle all night and morning.

So it was no surprise when I did finally wake, at noon, that my entire body groaned, especially my right hip and arm, since I had slept on that side, unmoving, for twelve hours. I rolled over onto my back and blinked at the ceiling, trying to figure out if I had dreamed the whole thing. Did I really just catch a killer and almost get beaned in the head for my efforts?

A knock at my door roused me, and I shuffled across the room to open it. It was Lois.

"I really hope you're not here to ask me to do you another favor. Because the last one I did nearly killed me."

She shook her head, stepped in, and wrapped me in her arms. I tried not to squeak in pain. I appreciated her hug, even if I had to bite down on my lip to stop from crying out. "Ginny told me everything that happened. You poor girl." She released me, thank God, and came into the suite to sit on the edge of the sofa. "What can I do for you?"

I followed her in and sat next to her. Scout immediately jumped up into my lap and started to purr. "Well, the next couple of days off would be nice."

"Done," she said.

"A spa day?"

"Done."

"A raise?"

Lois's eyes narrowed. "You've been here a week, Andi. Let's not go overboard." She stood, having completed the

business she came to do, and made her way to the door. I
followed her.

"Thanks, Lois, for checking in on me."

"Of course." She smiled and patted my undamaged cheek.
"Oh, while you have those days off, it will give you a chance to
get those cats boarded somewhere else."

I shut the door and padded back to the sofa to sit. For
every minute that passed, one muscle in my body stiffened. In
an hour, it was going to be like rigor mortis had settled in.
Happy that I didn't have to move for the rest of the day if I
didn't want to, I reached for my phone and checked my
messages. Surprise, surprise. In addition to the message from
my mother that I'd forgotten about, I had two missed calls
from Sheriff Jackson.

I checked my voice mail. The first message was from my
mother. It wasn't going to get any better if I kept ignoring her. I
pushed the button to hear what she had to say.

"We received your message, dear. We're sorry about your
job, but it's perfect timing. You know you're expected to take
your place here, in Hong Kong. Call me when you get this
message, and we'll make the arrangements."

Second message: "It's Sheriff Jackson. I'm calling to let you
know that Sasha Wilkes was released from custody. I told you I
would call."

Third message: "It's Sheriff Jackson. Again. I hope you are
feeling...okay. Better I mean. You don't need to call me back."

I ignored my mother. No way was I going to Hong Kong. I'd
told them that repeatedly in the years since they'd left me here
with Miss Charlotte and moved to the other side of the world.
The mere idea was a non-starter. The sooner they accepted my
decision, the better.

As for the sheriff, I chuckled and proceeded to dial his number.

"I said you didn't need to call me back," he said after picking up on the second ring.

"Well, you could've just let it go to voice mail."

"Right. So, how's your face?"

"It's fine. It will heal." I gently patted my cheek. It was still sore.

"Good."

"So…"

"Andi, I'm not going to discuss the case with you."

"Why not? I essentially solved it for you."

His sigh was loud, and I had to suppress a chuckle. It wouldn't do me any good to make him cranky. Crankier, I mean.

"Okay, just tell me this…how did she get into the spa? It was locked, and there was no back door."

"With a key."

I frowned, and then it hit me. "Mick, the maintenance guy, gave her a key. He also was the one that set out the sign that the pool was closed."

"Yeah. Looks like she paid him pretty good. Found him on a bender on the mainland. Turns out he used to work for her dad years ago." He cleared his throat. "I have to hang up now. Take care of yourself, Andi."

"I will."

"And stay out of trouble." He ended the call.

Chuckling, I set my phone down. The cats jumped up onto the sofa to get my attention. They likely sensed I needed the extra love.

"So, what should we do today?"

They both meowed.

"You're right. We should eat. I'm starving." I got up and went to the little kitchenette. I put food into two bowls for the cats and then opened the refrigerator to find something for me. The shelves were basically empty. My stomach growled, reminding me I hadn't eaten anything substantial in almost twenty-four hours. My options were to order room service or go down to the lobby and get something from the Lady Slipper Tea Room.

A lot had happened in the past few days. I started a new job, found a dead body, and basically solved the murder. I'd been busy. I looked around at the emptiness of my suite and decided a walk down to the lobby would do me some good. I got changed, carefully combed my hair—my scalp throbbed something fierce—put it into a messy bun, then headed to the lobby.

I passed the Chamber Crew along the way. They all stopped what they were doing and gave me a hug. Well, Nancy didn't, but I figured she wasn't much of a hugger.

"We heard what you did," Tina said. "You're kind of a hero."

"Not a hero. Just doing—" I'd almost said "my job," but instead I said, "what I thought was right."

"My dad said you're not that bright, running into danger like that." Megan snapped her gum. "But I think you're cool."

"Well, thanks." Was it stupid that my pride swelled at that a bit?

I continued to the lobby and imagined that Nicole was manning the concierge desk. She'd probably give me the stink eye the moment she saw me. As I rounded the corner, I was delighted to see Lane standing behind the big desk. He smiled and waved at me. I waved back. He looked overjoyed to be doing the job, and I wondered if I was going to have to worry about that. It was bad enough that I had to worry about the illustrious Casey Cushing.

Maybe I shouldn't have asked for those days off. Lois wouldn't do that to me, would she? She was turning out to be more cutthroat than I remembered her to be. What happened to the affable, loving mother from Kalamazoo who gave me silk pajamas with little puppies on them for Christmas one year? I was going to have to watch my butt around here. The hotel business was a lot more competitive than I'd assumed it would be.

I went into the tea house and ordered two paninis, a small garden salad, and some Kombucha to go. As I waited, I opened the bottle of tea and turned around. It sloshed over the rim again, but this time, it missed the pair of shiny black shoes behind me.

"You really should keep the lid on until you turn around." Daniel gave a little chuckle, although the humor didn't quite reach his eyes.

"Good advice. I'll take it into consideration for next time."

"I heard what happened." He became somber as he regarded me. His gaze took in the scratches to my face. I'd forgotten to look in a mirror before I left the room. "Are you okay?"

"Yeah, I'm good. All in a day's work."

He smiled. "Well, you're one hell of a concierge."

"I like to think so."

"I'm heading back to the mainland. I saw you from across the lobby and thought I'd come say goodbye."

"I hope you enjoyed your stay at the Park Hotel." I did a little curtsy. Which was really silly and over the top, but I was too tired and worn out to care much.

He reached into his inner suit jacket pocket and pulled out a business card. He handed it to me. "If you're ever on the mainland, give me a call."

"Sure." I slid the business card into the front pocket of my pants.

"Well, goodbye, Andi Steele."

"Goodbye, Daniel Evans."

He turned and left the shop just as my order was ready. Sighing, I grabbed my bag of food and went back to my room, shuffling my feet as I walked. I passed the corridor to the pool and spa and wondered if they'd opened both yet. I couldn't imagine Lois would keep them shut now that everything had been cleaned and the murderer arrested. Maybe I would just go take a peek and make sure. Maybe there was something I could help with.

Just as I was about to veer off in that direction, Ginny came around the opposite corner. "Andi? What are you doing up? I'd thought you would've slept all day."

"I got in twelve hours. That's enough." I lifted the food bag. "And I was hungry."

She had that knowing look in her eye, and I tried not to acknowledge it. I looked everywhere but at her. "You don't know what to do with yourself, do you?"

I shook my head. "No. I was just hungry."

"You could've ordered room service."

"Yeah but—"

She swung her arm around my shoulders. "Tell you what. You can help me cook the family meal tonight at Mom's cottage." She steered me away from the pool corridor and back toward my room. "Every Tuesday night, we all get together and eat and check in with each other. It was something my dad started, so we continue the tradition."

"Would I be welcome?"

"Yes. You're like family. You always have been."

"Okay. I'll be there."

CHAPTER FORTY-ONE

AT FOUR O'CLOCK, I arrived at Lois's cottage. It was a picturesque white house with green trim. Flowers of all colors and varieties grew in abundance around the whole place. Before I went to the door, I turned and looked out at the view over the cliff. I took in a deep breath of fresh air and smiled.

Despite the chaos of the past week, I was finally starting to feel at home here. I was still a fish out of water. But not quite so much the outsider. Maybe it was because of the chaos. Not sure. Ginny was likely right about me—I always had to be "into something."

As I thought about feeling at home, I remembered that I needed to write again to Miss Charlotte, give her the latest scoop—or at least parts of it. She wasn't my nanny anymore, but I still felt closer to her than my own mother.

The door behind me opened, and Lois stepped out. "Andi. I'm so glad Ginny thought to invite you."

"Are you sure it's okay?"

She opened her arms to me. "Of course. C'mon inside."

Ginny and I managed to put together a pretty decent meal of grilled whitefish, mashed potatoes, and side vegetables. My solo contribution was a blueberry pie, from a recipe I'd gotten from Miss Charlotte. Ginny set the table—Lois at the head, me and Ginny on one side, Eric and Nicole on the other. There was another place setting at the end of the table opposite Lois. It was where Henry had sat, and Lois insisted on putting a plate there to honor him. Ginny told me she did it at every meal.

When we all came to the table, Nicole gave me a quick smile, and I could feel the animosity radiating from her across the fine linen and the serving plate of whitefish. As Lois passed the dishes around, she talked about how the week went at the hotel. Of course, the biggest topic of conversation was the murder of Thomas Banks and the arrest of Pamela Bower.

Lois lifted her wineglass in a toast. "To Andi. If it hadn't been for you, they would've arrested the wrong person for the murder."

Everyone lifted their glasses. Even Nicole, except hers was barely off the tablecloth. As she took a sip of the red wine, she mumbled around the rim. I heard her plain as day, "Yeah, by bumbling across evidence. Doesn't take a genius to do that."

I smiled at her and resisted the urge to kick her under the table right in the shin with my pointy-toed shoes. "I'd like to thank all of you for opening your arms to me." I looked over at Ginny. "Not sure what I would've done if Ginny hadn't invited me to the island."

Nicole mumbled again with tight lips, "Get a job like everyone else."

"Well, we're very glad you're here," Eric said and raised his glass.

Nicole's head snapped to the side, and she gave him the deadliest of looks. I suspected there was going to be a grand old fight in their future. I felt bad for Eric. He was definitely woefully unprepared for Nicole's wrath.

I put my attention back on my food, not wanting to be a part of that squabble. The food was delicious, the company, for the most part, warm and inviting, and finally my shoulders drooped, and I was able to relax. I was still going for that promised spa day, though. A good massage was just what I needed to knead away the rest of my anxiety. I looked around at my new "family" and thought everything was going to be fine. I would make this work. I would learn to be happy here and make a go at being a fantastic concierge. Thinking of Daniel, maybe I'd even spark a new relationship. A girl could do a lot worse than the handsome mayor of Frontenac City.

While I was cutting the pie and putting pieces on plates, the door to the cottage opened, and an elderly man in a brown fedora walked in. He had a full head of white hair and trimmed white beard. His face had

the familiar pert nose and full lips that Ginny possessed.

Lois slowly got to her feet. "Dad? What are you doing here?"

He had to be Grandpa Samuel Park. Who else could he be?

The man took off his hat tossed it onto the vacant chair. He ran a hand over his white whiskers. "I'm here to find out what the heck is going on with my hotel and why there's a woman named Andi Steele trying to ruin it."

ABOUT THE AUTHOR

Diane Capri is an award-winning *New York Times*, *USA Today*, and world-wide bestselling author. She writes several series, including the Park Hotel Mysteries, the Hunt for Justice, Hunt for Jack Reacher, and Heir Hunter series, and the Jess Kimball Thrillers. She's a recovering lawyer and snowbird who divides her time between Florida and Michigan. An active member of Mystery Writers of America, Author's Guild, International Thriller Writers, Alliance of Independent Authors, and Sisters in Crime, she loves to hear from readers and is hard at work on her next novel.

Please connect with her online:

http://www.DianeCapri.com

Twitter: http://twitter.com/@DianeCapri

Facebook: http://www.facebook.com/Diane.Capri1

http://www.facebook.com/DianeCapriBooks

Made in the USA
Lexington, KY
27 October 2019

56148794R00148